FIRST-TIME COWBOY BODYGUARD

FIRST-TIME COWBOY BODYGUARD

A QUIET, SLOW-BURN PROTECTOR ROMANCE

ROUGH & READY PROTECTORS
BOOK ONE

ENGRID EAVES

EE PUBLISHING

TRIGGER WARNING

This book explores themes of emotional abuse, reclaiming autonomy, and healing after control, handled with care and centered on consent, agency, and love.

Please read at your own discretion.

JOIN THE ENGRID EAVES COMMUNITY!

ALPHA-EMOTIONAL HEROES.
HEADSTRONG, CURVY GIRLS.
SAVAGE ROMANCE.

GIVEAWAYS. FREEBIES.
NEW RELEASES. LATEST NEWS.

Subscribe to my newsletter today to never miss out on a
new steamy, small-town read.
SIGN UP FOR MY NEWSLETTER

PROLOGUE
MIA

Bright white lights flood the studio, and suddenly I feel smaller. On stage, there's space to move—the dark of night, places to roam. But here, I'm an ant under a magnifying glass.

My eyes dart to my mom and my manager, Edwin Crowe, just offstage. His gaze flicks to my hands. Heat crawls up his neck. I'm still holding the bag. The makeup artist was supposed to take it.

"We're here with Mia Love, America's favorite child pop star," the anchor's voice cuts through the thick thoughts swirling like alphabet soup in my head.

I clutch the bag tighter, hoping it's below the camera's sweep. Edwin's face simmers. Mom placates.

"And well, tell us what you're up to," the woman says, pausing mid-sentence—gingersnap-red hair, makeup perfectly predictable. Her eyes drop to the bag in my lap.

"Oh, these?" I giggle, lifting a small crocheted turtle. "They keep me busy on long road trips."

"That's right," she says too emphatically. "You're in the

middle of your current tour. Can you tell our audience more about it?"

Edwin's voice sears through my memory: *Put those stupid animals of yours down and focus.*

He thinks they make me look too childish. Mom says I should listen to him. He's my manager, my ticket to fame.

But what they don't know? The little animals make me feel sane—connected to the only person I miss. My grandma.

"Mia?" the anchor prompts, eyes catching mine.

"Oh," I chuckle, shaking my head. "My Grammy taught me how to crochet little forest critters." I lift a red fox. "This is Elmer. He sleeps with me at night. Protects me."

The anchor laughs a beat too long. "You can take the girl out of childhood," she says lightly, "but you can't take the childhood out of her."

I cock my head, unsure of what she means. My fingers fidget, brushing soft yarn.

"What I was asking about," she continues, "is your tour."

I shrug. Sleep. Eat. Perform. Travel. I shift on the stool.

Edwin's eyes shoot daggers. Mom shakes her head, a warning etched on her face. I try again, thinking harder this time. Remembering what we practiced before I stepped onto the *Good Morning USA* soundstage.

"It's the Sweet Thirteen Tour," I say. "Because I'm thirteen."

My foot taps the rung of the stool, hollow and nervous, until my manager's glower stills me.

Think, Mia, think.

"There are fireworks and loud music," I add brightly. "I sing all my fan favorites. It's a blast!"

The anchor's expression tightens, cinnamon freckles stark.

I shiver. *Did I say something wrong?*

"And school?" she asks. "Friendships?"

Everyone asks this. No one wants the truth.

My gaze drops to the animals in my lap—Oscar, Millie, Cindy. Sometimes, they're the only friends I have.

But nobody wants a sob story.

"I have a tutor," I recite. "And lots of friends."

My manager. My bodyguard. The roadies. My mom.

I flash my famous smile—the one I perfected before I finished losing my baby teeth.

"Well," the anchor says, "it sounds like you stay busy."

"I do." I lift my chin.

"Do you have a favorite song to perform?"

I pause—just long enough to tease. Just like my acting coach taught me.

"Anything off my latest album *Hello, Sunflower*."

"Well timed," the anchor says curtly. "As we take a commercial break, here's the title track by Miss Mia Love."

The cameras cut away. My shoulders drop.

The anchor goes cold as a makeup artist brushes over her plastic smile.

Edwin and Mom rush me. Dad left so long ago I have trouble remembering his face.

Before I can react, Edwin snatches the crocheted animals. Hands them to my mom with a derisive snort. "Keep your kid under control, Mom."

She stuffs them in her purse, eyes darting between Edwin and me.

"These silly things again. I should throw them away," she whispers, face ambivalent.

She never takes my side. She always takes *his*.

3

"No." The word comes out too loud. The studio shifts—every head turning. "Please."

"Mia," Mom raises an eyebrow. "You're here to make and sell music. Nothing else."

She lingers, caught between me and Edwin, who paces a distance away, screaming into his cell phone.

"We have to keep him happy, Mia," Mom adds, frowning. Just for a while longer. Just until we have enough money to stand on our own two feet.

"Why did Dad have to leave?" I whine, a single tear cascading down my cheek.

She tut-tuts with her tongue, wiping it away. "Don't make the makeup artist come back over here," she scolds.

I bite my bottom lip until I taste blood, twisting my hands in my lap.

When the lights flare again, and the cameras roll, I become her.

Mia Love.

America's favorite child pop star.

A brand.

Not a girl.

CHAPTER
ONE
MIA

Eight years later, the crowd is screaming my name.

Bass shakes the floor. Heat presses in. The lights are no longer blinding. They're mine.

My makeup artist's brush stops mid-air. Sylvia straightens, mouth quirked in concentration, her pixie-cut red hair trembling with the chaos onstage. The Cherry Picks, the opening band, wail the last lines of their encore.

"Ready to show Rough & Ready Country how it's done?"

I chuckle, cocking my head. "Not sure if that's possible. This place is..." *How do I put it nicely?* "Off the beaten path."

"And filled with adorable cowboys. Have you looked out at your audience?" she asks, drawing closer, cheeks flushed and voice vibrating with excitement.

"Had my fill of those by Nashville and Houston," I lie, corners of my mouth turning down.

"Unlike you, Mia, I don't think I'll ever get enough."

I don't doubt her for one moment.

The gray suits circle, and Sylvia steps back, eyes darting to mine for one breathless moment.

Edwin says, his tone nasal. "Your parents' extra security is ... underfoot." He looks down his nose at one large man with a military bearing. "Shall I say overkill?"

I shrug.

"Still no clue what got into them?" he asks, eyes scrutinizing me. "Estranged for years, and now they suddenly care—*conveniently*?"

"Who knows?" I answer, tired of him posing questions I can't answer. "Could be their little way of saying 'sorry for abandoning you.'"

His eyebrows waggle.

My stomach knots, and I lick my bottom lip, eyeing my parents' unexpected contribution to tonight's show. A wall of cowboy hats, muscle, grim faces, and shiny boots and buckles—the last thing I need. One man steps forward, jaw sharp enough to cut glass, eyes narrow and steely.

"Boone. I'm lead."

My eyes glance past him to the crew. One guy's got dark blond hair and moss green eyes, striking against his tanned skin. A snake tattoo wraps around his arm, beading perspiration in the heat of the Nevada evening. Another—tall, intimidating, with a short beard—frowns, tattoos peeking from the V of his button-down. But it's the man next to them—lethal, quiet—who I remember.

Ebony hair, earth-toned eyes, quietly watchful. A well-trimmed beard and mustache frame his angular face, and high-cut, sculpted cheekbones seem almost too intentional for his rugged face. Like his lips—too perfect for me to stop staring, though I never should've started.

Edwin clears his throat, and I come back to it all. The dry heat of the Great Basin night, the dust hanging in the air, thick like the tension before taking the stage. Boots pound the ground, the crowd chanting, "Mia! Mia!"

"Thank you for your help tonight," I say curtly to Boone, wheeling around so my back faces him and his team. No point fraternizing with the paid help. I've seen far too many faces to remember names. Besides, if I were being honest—if I were allowed to give my real opinion—I'd admit to uneasiness about the extra brawn tonight. Everyone in this business knows additional security means trouble.

My eyes snag on the man with black hair, though his eyes never meet mine. Too cold. Too aloof. Yet, something about the cut of his jaw, the way he stands cagey and confident, ebbs away lingering anxiety.

Edwin grabs my elbow, pulling me to the side. "Received notice from the legal team about somebody who's been sniffing around, asking too many questions."

"Oh, yeah?"

"Know anything about it, Tiger."

Tiger. I hate that nickname.

I ask, "What are you implying?"

"Shhh," he says, raising his hands. "No need to make a scene. I just need to know whose side you're on."

"My own," I say by rote.

He cracks a smile. "And who's on your side?" He smiles. "The only one in your corner?"

I sigh, the words muscle memory more than anything I consciously believe. "You, Edwin. Always you."

"Don't forget it." He pauses, eyes drilling into me. "Because without me, this business would eat you alive."

"I know," I say, only half-listening. We've had this conversation so many times, I could deliver it in my sleep. Only something about it is more urgent tonight.

"I mean, just your recent weight gain alone, Mia. You're no easy cookie to manage."

"Hey—" I start.

"He's not wrong," Lawrence butts in, my PR manager. His eyes sweep up and down my scantily clad frame for one long, devastating moment. "Some things you can't cover with makeup."

I bite my bottom lip until I taste it—salty and metallic, the edge of my reason.

"Just remember," Edwin says, the creases in his forehead deepening, "every place I've given you autonomy, your life's a fucking mess. Expanding freedom, expanding waistline."

"You sure know how to give a pre-concert pep talk."

His smile is colder than a glacier. "Go get 'em, Tiger."

AN HOUR INTO THE CONCERT, my halter top clings to my ribs, sticky with sweat. Perspiration pours from my bandmates, and my backup dancers look like they're in the middle of a wet T-shirt contest.

"Gotta hand it to y'all," I say into the mic to a deafening roar of applause, "You sure know how to do hot down here. Big and bold, like everything about this state. Ready for an oldie but a goodie?"

Behind me, the band cuts into the opening strains of *Hello, Sunflower*. Screams fill the air, piercing, deafening. Diehard fans stand out, faces red and glistening with enthusiasm.

My eyes dart to the left-hand side of the stage where the man with black hair stands—still. Watchful. Unmoving in a way that feels deliberate.

I grip the microphone, launching into the opening verse, and the crowd sings along. An anthem to anyone who's ever felt lonely, like they don't fit in. An anthem to kids who grew up too fast and lived too hard.

My mind goes blank, like it always does. It's the only way I get through the same performances again and again. Different cities, different time zones, always the same crowds demanding everything from me—far more than I have to give.

In the center of the crowd, working his way to the front. I catch sight of a lone man parting the crowd. His face is dark—shadowed in a way that goes beyond lighting—his eyes intent and intense. I watch him snaking through, people pulling back. The air feels electric. Gasps shiver through the crowd. Like everyone's collectively holding and releasing their breath.

Then, a scream. One piercing sound, though my eyes never break from the man now at the front of the stage. It all happens so quickly my brain can't catch up. A sudden movement. A flash of steel.

A hard body crashes into me, and I hit the stage hard, music still thumping, crowd yelling—not in adoration but panic.

Pop! Pop! Pop!

A concussive sound shreds the air, muted by the heavy body covering mine.

"You okay?" A deep voice growls.

I stare into dark eyes. "Y-y-yes."

The gaze narrows, hand coming to the wire in his ear, listening. "Asset secure. Awaiting extraction."

I can barely breathe, body buried beneath the weight of the cowboy bodyguard. Voices shrill, the music dead now, but the sound of gunfire still piercing the air.

Each burst sends another tremble through my core.

"You able to move?" the man asks.

I nod, bottom lip trembling, tongue frozen.

"Copy," he says to whatever voice is behind the wire.

Suddenly, he jumps to his feet, pulling me with him. "Move, move, move."

But my knees buckle, my body paralyzed.

He eyes me wildly, then sweeps me into his arms and sprints toward the stage exit. I wrap my arms around his neck, breath coming fast, heart outpacing my pulse.

Offstage, his eyes sear into me, heat rolling off them ... or perhaps anger.

"When I tell you to move, you fucking move," he screams, setting me back on my feet.

No one's spoken to me like this before, especially not a bodyguard. But the fear in his voice isn't about control—it's about losing me. Concern etches his face, raw and unguarded, louder than anything he can say.

I nearly fall when he tries to let me go, his grip the only thing keeping me upright.

"You wounded and didn't tell me?" he grunts, eyes and hands sliding slowly over me.

"No," I manage, hands still gripping his neck. "But don't let go of me. Not yet."

TWO

MAVERICK

The suited guys come over—the ones who've given me the creeps ever since we got here.

"She's okay?" Edwin Crowe asks. Something about the tone of his voice, the look on his face, gets a permanent spot in my memory.

I've observed the talkative man more than I care to since arriving on this job. No insults or shouting. No cruelty in tone. He speaks like an HR rep or a lawyer. He gives off the air of a concerned caretaker around the main act, Mia Love.

Everything about him is inauthentic. Fake as fuck. Thin-framed and gracile, eyes sharp as a vulture's beak—watching, waiting. But words precise enough to cut.

Crowe doesn't raise his voice. He doesn't threaten. He just ... waits.

And people act scared shitless around him. Because what he represents—success, fame, the music industry—is far more terrifying than any one man could be.

"Need to move her fast. Get her safe," I grunt.

"We can take it from here—"

I grimace, eyeing the men. Something about this isn't right.

Boone's voice blasts in my ear. "Shooter down. Local PD taking perimeter. EMS staging. Holt, you still have eyes on the asset?'

More like arms locked around her. "Asset safe and secure," I reply.

"Good," my boss grits between clenched teeth.

The woman in my arms shakes, her perspiration-kissed body melting against mine. She grips me like a fucking lifeline in shark-infested waters. My eyes meet hers, a question on my lips.

But I already know the answer. She's not ready to stand alone yet, to feel the weight of it all. So, I hold the space with her, let reality sink in slowly.

"Don't let me go," she whispers, staring up at me. And then, there's what she doesn't say. The disparaging look toward the suits. Like her eyes plead, *Don't leave me with them*.

I should say something. But I'm no good at that.

Instead, I nod. Nodding's never gotten me in trouble.

AN HOUR LATER, R&R Security debriefs with the police. My arms still feel warm where Mia Love filled them. I try not to think about it, though my gaze sneaks her direction more than once. I catch her watching me back.

"Thanks to Holt here," Boone says, drawing my attention back. I grunt, setting my jaw. "Wouldn't advise taking down an asset that abruptly. But a concussion's better than bullet holes."

I shrug, my cheeks heating, though I don't know why.

"Yeah," Knox cuts in, green eyes snapping, "you were giving off NFL vibes—not PBR ones."

Mia's face is a question as she silently mouths *PBR*. Totally clueless. But what do I expect from a big city, Hollywood type?

"Bulls or bullets. All the same to me," I grumble, never one for good one-liners.

The woman steps closer, face taut, listening.

Boone's eyes cut between us, settling on her flushed cheeks. "Sure you don't want to get checked out by the paramedics?"

She shakes her head, raising her chin resolutely. "No one was injured," she whispers, voice threaded with awe. Like she cares more about her audience than herself. Like she doesn't fit the mold. She hugs herself, body still trembling. "And I'm fine. So, no."

I fight the urge to pull her close, let my flesh eat her fear. But she's my asset, for God's sake. Can't look soft in front of the crew, especially on my first job.

"Looks like you're off the hook," Beckett chimes in, quieter than the rest, eyes tracking the room. "No concussion means job security."

Boone's jaw tenses, silently correcting Beckett.

"Your man saved me," Mia cuts in, looking at Boone like she expects him to do or say something. "Rough or not."

I shift uneasily. Don't need acknowledgment. Don't need recognition. "Part of the job."

"Any idea who might have it out for you?" Boone asks, removing his Stetson and running his fingers through his hair.

She shrugs. Something about the gesture makes her look fragile, tiny. My eyes dart back to the men in suits, lingering around the edge of the backstage crowd like hungry lions.

Edwin steps forward again, slimy, slippery. The kind of man I despise. "Likely just a crazed fan. She gets lots of those, you know."

"A stalker," she says, lips pressing into a thin line. "I collect those the way some girls do handbags."

He nods. "Fortunately, he's in custody now. No one was hurt, and you can get back to what you do best."

"No," she says firmly.

Edwin's mouth curves. "No's not in the contract, Tiger."

"I told you. I need a break. I need—"

The air tightens. Even the suits stop moving.

She continues, "Not after a shooting at my concert. No, I won't do another show until..."

"Until?" his eyes narrow, the pupils black and glistening.

"Until I have time to think things through. Think about what needs to change."

"Wait, what?"

"What needs to change," she hisses. "Like security. If my parents hadn't..." Her voice falters. "If R&R Security hadn't been here, I don't even want to think about what could've happened. And as for your security detail. They were supposed to have every entrance covered tonight. They had metal detectors. This wasn't supposed to happen."

"Whoa. Hold up for a minute. Are you trying to blame this on me?" Edwin snaps.

My hands ball at my sides. Never cared much for men who intimidate women. I step forward.

"Ms. Love, R&R Security would be more than happy to

provide temporary protection, if you'd like?" Boone offers. "At least until all of this can be sorted out."

Edwin's face simmers.

Mia looks like a weight has lifted. "Really? You'd do that for me?"

Boone nods, eyeing Edwin skeptically. "Got a daughter who's a huge fan—"

"Wait, is she here tonight?" Mia butts in, eyes rounding.

"She begged," Boone admits. "But I said no."

"Thankfully."

He shrugs. "Been in this business long enough to know better."

She nods.

"Figure some merch and an autograph or two should settle up the cost of our services," he adds.

"Oh, I can pay," she says, face darkening when Edwin clears his throat.

"Actually—"

Boone cuts him off again. "No need. Might ask for a testimonial later, though."

"Deal," she says, face beaming. "But only if I have a say in who protects me."

"Of course." Boone nods.

A low laugh rumbles beside me, and the quiet one shifts —all eyes on me.

"This one's who I want," she says, eyeing me like a prize stallion she just won at auction.

Fuck. First assignment. Worst complication possible.

"This newbie?" Amos chides in, his laughter a low boom.

"Newbie?" Mia asks, and my shoulders drop a little, relief in sight.

15

"Yes," Boone says with a nod. "Tonight's his first assignment. If you'd like somebody with a little more experience—"

"Nope, I've seen more than enough to know. If he's already this good, I'm in safe hands."

"If you don't end up with a concussion," the quiet one grumbles.

"Yeah, no more tackling her, Rookie. Alright, let's get back to command and sort everything out. Ms. Love, you're coming with us. Anything you need to bring along, Holt can grab for you."

"Holt?" she asks imperiously, arching a perfectly groomed eyebrow.

"Maverick Holt," I say.

She cocks her head to the side, eyes taking me in from head to toe like I'm a living, breathing commodity.

"Mia Love," she says with the kind of smile that could break open a rawhide heart. Fortunately, that part of my anatomy quit working when my rodeo career ended.

I grimace, then, look away. "Not much of a talker. But safety. That I can do."

"Sounds like the beginning of a beautiful friendship."

The crew laughs, and I fold my arms, frowning. Not enough pay in the world for *this*.

The pop star's eyes snap to Boone. "Let's go meet your daughter."

"Wait." Edwin steps between us, irritation animating his face. "You are not allowed to go with these men. You are not allowed to make agreements without—"

Anger flares. I push between them. "Ms. Love's spoken."

I glower.

He caves.

Mia's body relaxes.

16

"She'll be in touch when she's ready."

"This isn't how these things usually end," he says quietly. "You're going to regret this."

I glare.

Edwin narrows his eyes, then he turns and strides away, the rest of the suits following like a pack of hyenas.

THREE

MIA

I ron, wood, and stone greet us as we pass through a massive gate, headlights illuminating the billowing dust clouds kicked up in the train of black Ford F-350s that make their way to R&R Security's headquarters.

"Is it pretty during the day?" I ask, shifting uneasily in the passenger seat next to Maverick.

He side-eyes me, too intense, a low sound—almost a growl—humming from his chest.

I finger the hem of my black floral sundress, hands fidgeting nervously. I want something to hold, something to comfort me.

Country music blares. My hand comes up to adjust the station, but the big man shoots me a warning glare.

"Really?" I glance at the radio. "Your way or the highway when it comes to music?"

The corners of his mouth tip down.

I chuckle, staring at my tangled fingers. "What you did back there—" I look up, but his eyes never leave the road. "Covering me like that ... risking your life. I can't begin to—"

"No need."

Minutes tick by.

"So, today was your first day on the job? And already dodging bullets..."

I shift again, and the leather seat squeaks. "You said something earlier. Bulls or bullets. What did you mean?"

His hands grip the steering wheel tighter.

I cross my arms. "You know, this is going to be boring as hell if you refuse to talk."

Silence.

"Fortunately, I have plenty to say. I basically never stop talking, according to Edwin and the other gray suits. I'm silly, loudmouthed, superficial—only good for entertainment. What do you think about that?"

He grunts, pulling up in front of a large two-story structure. He jumps out, slamming the driver's door. Rounding the front of the truck, he opens mine, hand outstretched to help me out of the boosted vehicle.

I'm used to riding in limos with tailored drivers. Not launching myself out of all-terrain vehicles. I'm used to polite nods and formal greetings, not a calloused hand that trails sparks of heat up my arm. Not a man who smells of pine sap and something darker, almost primitive.

He keys a code. We pass through a doorway into a maze of cinderblock rooms like something out of a CIA training video.

Not so much a ranch—more like a compound.

The second story is open air, metal gangways crisscrossing above, a solid roof overhead to keep out the weather. It should be intimidating. Instead, the quiet is safety, order.

Maverick strides ahead, his body rather than his words telling me to follow. We meet in a sparsely furnished office with light knotty pine-lined walls and aviation-inspired images on the walls. Boone takes a seat behind a large wooden desk as the men gather chairs, offering me one in the middle.

A black clock ticks on the wall, ten fifty-three p.m. My concert should be wrapping up right about now. Instead, I'm surrounded by dangerous-looking men. Despite the late hour, dry heat presses against my flesh as Boone makes a phone call.

"We're at the Ranch."

Four words, and he ends the call. What is it with these guys? It's like they're hellbent on taking "strong and silent" to a whole new level.

I swallow hard, suddenly second-guessing every part of this plan. I glance toward Maverick, the awkward car ride still front and center. Not sure if I can deal with that again.

But Edwin's threats, his expression, compel me to wait this out. I've finally bought myself a respite. A little peace. A moment of reflection. I can't turn back now.

"My sister and pipsqueak are on the way. Hope you're ready to make a little girl's dream come true," Boone says, leaning back in his chair.

"Part of the job," I parrot back, mimicking Maverick. If he notices, he doesn't give it away. But then again, the man's got a poker face like no other.

I lick my bottom lip, hands twisting in my lap. "Am I going to stay here?" My voice comes out like a squeak, though I don't mean to sound ungrateful.

"It's no Hyatt," the green-eyed man cuts in, comments few but sharp.

"Having second thoughts, Ms. Love?" Boone asks.

I take a deep breath, letting it out slowly. "No, it's just..."

The security lead's eyebrows raise, and he leans forward.

My head bobs around the room, words evading me. "It's just so quiet here." I pause, crickets and katydids a deafening choir despite my words. But that's not what I'm talking about.

"I get it," the cowboy says, removing his Stetson, and setting it on the desk. "But you said you wanted a break. We can give that to you ... temporarily."

It's what I asked for—space, silence—but now that I have it, I don't know what to do with it.

Outside, a truck engine grows louder, then it cuts.

"We'll do a debrief tomorrow morning. Any questions?" He eyes the silent room.

Two female voices echo through the compound. A moment later, they fill Boone's office, and the energy in the room shifts. Thank goodness.

A wide-eyed preteen with dirty blonde hair and big brown eyes stands awestruck, unmoving, unblinking. At her elbow is a plump woman with chestnut-colored locks, cheeks flushed, eyes dancing.

"Mia Love." The girl says it like she's seeing a ghost or maybe a genie freshly sprung from a lamp.

I rise, clasping my hands together and smiling warmly. "And you must be Josie. I've heard so much about you from your dad."

Her eyes skim past me to Boone, and warmth crowds my chest. Suddenly, she breaks into a song and dance— *Hello, Sunflower*. I join in until we both laugh.

"Hey, you're not half bad. Ever thought about heading out on the road as one of the Lovettes?" I tease, referring to my backup dancers.

"Oh," Josie exclaims, gaze locking on her dad.

"No way," he grumbles, rising and circling the desk to take the place next to his daughter, ruffling her hair.

Those two words, the affectionate way they interact, do something to me. I could never imagine my dad treating me like this ... or caring enough to say no when it matters.

A dangerous sting hits the back of my eyes, and I glance away for a moment, breathing slowly.

Maverick doesn't miss the gesture.

"So, how about we look through merch and sign stuff?" I ask.

"Sign stuff?" She puts her hand over her heart.

"Lots of stuff. Whatever you'd like," I answer with a broad grin. "I'm here to make this memorable."

The glimmer in her eyes lets me know I've already exceeded the goal.

But Boone's expression is more ambivalent, like he's weighing the cost of this interaction. Wondering if it's healthy for his little girl.

I choke up a little at his protectiveness, excusing it away as nerves from tonight. But inside, I wonder how different my life might have been if I'd had a dad like Boone. All I know for sure is protection is quieter than I expected.

CHAPTER

FOUR

MAVERICK

"There's only one bed." She says it like it *matters*. Like I can't handle the rougher side of life.

"That's right, Princess."

"Princess? Why do you call me that?"

Is she really asking me this? The list off the top of my head is enough to fill a novel. I appraise her perfectly manicured pink nails, long buttery locks, soft green eyes, thick, fake lashes, and face slathered in makeup, the corners of my mouth twitching.

Instead of speaking, I search the cabin for extra blankets and pillows. Wouldn't be the first night I spent on the ground. I've crashed here since arriving in town for the job, still not set on a place to call my own.

She gasps. "Wait, you can't sleep on the floor."

"Can and will."

"But why?"

I stop, folding my arms tightly over my chest. "'Cause you won't."

"Sleep on the floor? Never!"

23

I grunt, vindicated. The blankets hit the floor uncere-moniously, followed by the pillows. Good enough for me.

"But..."

I lift an eyebrow.

She shakes her head.

"Want a drink?" I ask—already regretting the question. Her pink glitter eyeshadow screams party girl.

I head to the kitchen, checking the cupboards. Stacked shot glasses and tequila greet me. I close the door quickly, but she's already noticed.

"Tequila shots?" she asks.

Great, the last thing she needs.

I frown.

Her face falls. "Joking, actually. What I really want is tea."

"Seriously?"

She nods. "Got any chamomile floating around up there?"

I snort, turning my back and rifling through a stash of loose-leaf teas in various metal containers. "No chamomile. But there's apple caramel, lavender blueberry—"

"Lavender blueberry," she cuts in, then yawns.

I fill the kettle with water and place it on the stove.

"Tired?"

I don't know why I ask. It's not like I want to have a conversation. But I can't deny something about this woman —about what happened earlier at the stadium—that makes me feel a connection.

"Exhausted," she says, snagging a blanket from the floor and wrapping it around her shoulders. Great, now it's going to smell like her—all floral and mouthwatering.

"Should I turn the a/c down?" I ask.

Mia shakes her head, though goosebumps line her

forearms. Pulling a stool up to the kitchen bar, she rests her elbows on the counter. "Not like I get shot at every day ... thankfully. Guess the adrenaline got to me or something."

Adrenaline used to be what I lived for.

Now, it's just a means to an end—income.

"Don't let me keep you from a drink," she says.

I shrug. "On the clock."

"True," she says, cocking her head. "But if anyone deserves a stiff one tonight, it's you."

I nod my agreement, then pull a second mug from the cabinet. Two teas, it is.

When I turn back, she's gripping her phone. Reading something. Face ashen in the faint glow from the screen.

"Something wrong?" I ask.

She startles. It tells me everything I need to know. "Just Edwin texting. Again."

"And?"

She shakes her head. "Not worth the time to explain it."

My gaze drills into her, noticing tells, subtle changes in her expression. "He just... He just won't understand that I need some time to think—alone."

"You're not asking too much," I remind.

She shrugs.

"Tell it to the gray suits. They want their commissions, their cuts. Can't accept the gravy train shutting down for a few days."

I shift, put my hands on my hips. "They're gonna have to."

She chuckles, like I've said something funny.

"You're the star, after all."

Mia twists her hands together atop the table. Like she needs to do something with them. Her heel thuds softly against the rung of the stool, her eyes staring at the walls until she's a million miles away.

"Star," she murmurs. "Such a loaded word."

I can't help but sneak a second glance at her. Still nervous, movements fast and stilted as a hummingbird, but her face is more relaxed, more authentic, the performer momentarily gone.

"Honey?" I ask, lifting the amber jar.

She startles, mossy eyes darting to my face. "That another nickname?"

Then, her eyes drop to the sweetener. She giggles. "A little."

I push the mugs across the counter, taking the stool across from her. Body rigid, eyes in constant line of sight of the door and windows just in case.

"Thought for sure you were a party girl." It slips out.

"Me, a party girl?" She giggles as if I've said something funny.

I nod slowly, waiting for her to speak. Silence never fails to coax something out of her.

"Oh, you mean because of the celebrity status?" She shakes her head. "Edwin would never let me do any of that." She surveys the room, shoulders drooping. "Any of this, either."

I want to ask her more, to find out what's going on with those vultures. The way they circled her, the way they stared. Like she's their meal ticket or something. But it's not my place. Instead, I stare ahead, hands wrapped around the warm ceramic mug.

"Josie was adorbs. Did you see how excited she got?" Mia says into her mug, blowing on the steaming liquid.

I let the silence do the talking.

"She knew all my songs by heart. And the dances. It was really, really cute."

"Cute? Not sure Boone thought so."

She straightens, side-eyeing me. "So, I'm not the only one who got that impression?"

I nod.

"He's right, you know." Her voice trails off.

"Right?"

"About keeping Josie away from that life, that world. She should have better role models than me."

"Maybe." I know how she feels. Too many boys look up to bull riders, too.

"Fame ... isn't what it's cracked up to be."

"You can say that again."

Her forehead knits, curiosity flashing.

I've said enough already. Maybe too much. "Tea okay?"

"Yes, thank you."

Crickets and katydids hum outside. A lone owl hoots, eerie and hollow.

Mia's face cracks into a grin. "Oh, did you hear that? I love owls."

Something tightens low in my chest.

"Can we go outside? Do you think the stars are visible?"

Her question floors me. There's only one answer. I remind myself I'm dealing with a city girl.

I shrug, grab my mug, and head for the door. Mia follows with a swish of soft skirts and fruity perfume.

She stands on the last porch step, gripping the railing and looking up. "Wow! This is amazing."

I shrug, tilting my head heavenward. Don't know about amazing. It's every night out here.

She hugs herself, eyes delighting at the glittering

swatch of diamond overhead. "So, how'd you become a bodyguard?"

"Plans changed." I don't want to get into it. Get into the injury that gutted my life and my career.

Mia laughs, shaking her head.

"What?"

"Questioning you makes me feel like I'm a CIA agent or something. Do I need to waterboard you to get a straight answer?"

I shrug. "Not much of a talker."

"You should tell me to sit down before major revelations like that. Last thing I want is to faint from shock."

I step forward, scanning the ground for what I need. Dipping low, I snag a perfectly smooth pebble, pale gray in the full moon's light, oblong and more flat than long. Unceremoniously, I pocket it.

"Don't tell me you're a rockhound."

She's funny, I'll give her that.

"Or," she says, tapping her finger against her lip. "Maybe you like skipping rocks across the river?"

I survey the vast expanse of valley surrounding the cabin, eyes searching the trees for movement, signs of anything out of place. Law enforcement may have taken a man into custody tonight, but that doesn't mean I'm off duty.

"Wait, is there even a river around here for skipping?" Our eyes meet, electricity sizzling for one moment before I look away.

Nope, Holt. Not now. Not ever.

"I could spend hours out here," she says, eyes drooping.

I fight the urge to ask if she's sure about that. The less talking we do, the better. Need to keep things impersonal, professional.

The curvy blonde's arms lift in a stretch indulgent enough for a cat. "But this night sky's putting me to sleep."

As it should.

She turns back toward the house, blanket pulled more tightly around her, and I watch the graceful dance of her skirt as she heads inside, and I follow. At the window by the front door, I pause, setting the flat rock on the sill just in case. A peace offering to Owl.

CHAPTER
FIVE
MAVERICK

orning starts before dawn. Blankets folded, neatly piled on the couch. Pillows beside them. I roll through surveillance footage from the perimeter, pore over camera hits.

A stray coyote, head tipping up curiously, ears wide for one moment before it drops its shoulders and scurries away. A badger on the south edge of the fence line, eyes glinting in grainy black-and-white. Two does, leisurely grazing the south pasture and taking advantage of the moonlit night.

But no sign of danger. No unexplained traffic.

Before I leave the cabin, I confirm the interior lights are operational and the doors locked. Then, I check the generator.

With thermos in hand, I drive the perimeter, jumping out and surveying blind spots between the cameras. I twist the cap, take a swig of the black, bitter liquid. No disturbed ground, no unaccounted for prints except those of two does, one of the badger in question, and another set of coyote.

All quiet. All clear.

A blonde-haired woman with eyes like soft moss slips into my mind.

I climb back in the truck, pushing thoughts of the curvy beauty from my mind.

Not professional, Holt. Not advisable.

Boone answers on the first ring, voice gruff.

"Site secure. No anomalies. Static perimeter."

"You get any sleep last night, Holt?"

"Sleep's overrated." Only the ache deep in my hip says otherwise. Stiffer than usual, trying to make me limp when I don't want it to.

He grunts. I end the call.

The Great Basin flies by the window. Stark and unforgiving. Like the look on Edwin's face.

My stomach twists, mind nudging me back to the way they looked at her. Their reaction when she was safe. How Edwin glowered when she requested a break. Time alone.

Back at the cabin, I check the window locks, then the maps. Remind myself of possible access routes. Areas that might need extra surveillance or tightening. Not that I need to do any of this.

Boone calls two hours later, confirming law enforcement received a confession.

Still, I plan. Because you never know.

Scrolling through lists, I sort information about Mia. Not sure what I'm looking for. My eyes rest on a YouTube video from eight years prior. I drop the volume on my laptop to a whisper, watching the footage of an awkward teen. Couldn't be much more than Josie's age. Funny how time alters life.

Eight years ago.

For me, that was the top of the world. But that's not what I pull up.

Instead, it's six months ago. My gut roils, a cold sweat breaking out on my forehead. The smell of cow manure, the shock waves of the bull moving beneath me. My hand slipping. And then—hooves and blood, mud and the unending spiral into oblivion.

Into this time and place. This fucking job ... *and Mia*.

The last part feels like a whisper ... because I can't let it be more.

I rub my hip, remembering pain in waves of loss rather than palpable sensation.

Newspaper articles float across the screen like phantoms.

Devastating injuries. A career cut short. The end of Maverick Holt...

That about sums it up.

A rustle of fabric, the swish of curls against flannel, bare feet padding across wood floors. I look up.

Mia Love.

She looks smaller today. Saner. Normal.

A flash of green through the squint of her eyes, like they haven't gotten the memo she's awake. I stand, enjoying far too much the way she stretches in the sun.

"Coffee?"

"Yes." It comes out like a growl.

I arch an eyebrow. "Not a morning person."

"God, no," she says, flopping onto a stool and burying her head in her arms atop the counter. She's positioned away from the glass. Good.

Her golden locks frame her head like a halo, the smell of plums and roses wafting through the air.

"And you?" she asks, sheepishly raising her head. Her

eyes descend to the neat stack of blankets and pillows, face glowing with guilt.

"Better than you."

She laughs. "Are you always this funny, Mav?"

The sarcastic question catches me so off guard the corners of my mouth turn up before I can stop them.

"A smile?" she asks with a wicked grin. "Am I finally getting through to you?"

I furrow my brow and tighten my face.

"I'll take that as a no."

She's starting to understand me. How I communicate. It lodges a weird warm spot behind my ribs.

But then, her cell phone buzzes again. She opens her screen, face falling.

"Crowe again?"

She sighs heavily, nodding. "Too early for this."

I want to state the obvious. That she should put the phone away. Go a day without charging it. But it's not my place.

Instead, I push the mug of coffee toward her.

She pockets the phone, fingers trembling. Like she has to keep the instrument of psychological torture close, sharp. Her shoulders stay tense even after the phone disappears.

"Cream? Sugar?"

"Nope. Princess is fine," she says without missing a beat.

I freeze.

She winks.

I frown. "Black, then."

"Actually, two tablespoons of creamer, no sugar. Keto style because my manager says I'm fat."

I lean back on my heels, words coming before I can stop myself. "Not fat."

"Not fat?" She looks down, pinching her waist through the yellow and black flannel shirt she wears. Mine. Don't know when she snagged it. But it's got me thinking thoughts I shouldn't.

"Curvy," I correct.

I return to my spot behind the kitchen counter, arms crossed, expression unreadable.

She swirls her coffee in the mug. "Curvy. Is that bad or good?"

"None of my business."

She snorts, looks away. "That answer shouldn't surprise me."

I shift my weight.

"But would it surprise you if I admitted something?"

I don't answer.

"If I admitted I want it to be your business?"

I take a swig of my coffee, trying to ignore the question.

"Still nothing to say?"

Mia lets out a defeated sigh. "You're no fun at all." Then, she stares into her coffee like it'll grow legs and run away.

"Never said I was."

"Never said much of anything." Mia's eyes narrow.

My cell phone vibrates in my pants pocket. I pull it out, see it's from Boone. "Better take this outside."

Mia nods, eyes dropping back to her mug.

34

CHAPTER

SIX

MIA

The second cup of coffee swirls with angry clouds of cream when the front door swings wide and Maverick enters again.

Wordless, expressionless, but with a slight limp I hadn't noticed before. Could be from sleeping on the floor. Could be something else entirely.

"How'd your call go?"

His face darkens. "Tell me about your manager. His crew."

I run my hands over my face, thoughts twisting and turning. Where to start? What to say?

"Why are you asking?"

His eyes narrow, face grim as he takes the stool next to me, turning so our knees are just an inch apart. "He says he has guardianship over you." His jaw tightens. "That true?"

The air escapes my lungs. My eyes cast down to the ground, and I reflexively feel the phone in my pocket. Heavier than it should be. Like it carries the weight of the world. I take a deep breath, steel myself. But I can't make the words come out. Instead, I nod.

"Why didn't you tell me sooner?"

I shrug, swallowing hard. My hands twist and turn in my lap now, like the thoughts in my head.

"I—I didn't think he'd stoop so low, didn't think he'd go there..."

I wait for the scolding tones, the judgmental glare. Instead, I find an open face and quiet strength, inviting me to speak.

My hands shake, and I can't find the words. My breath hitches as I try once, then again. "A couple of years back, I was so depressed. So done with all of it. The road, the concerts, the unending control. I wanted out. I wanted to take my money and run. But it was never that simple."

How do I say this without making myself sound pathetic?

"I thought about ... ending things. Not because I wanted to hurt myself but because I wanted so badly to escape the life that was carved out for me. To stop being Mia Love."

His mouth twitches like he's going to speak. Instead, he waits until I can't bear the silence a moment longer.

"They made me go to the doctor ... to a therapist. They got a diagnosis, and they got prescriptions. Things I had to take. They convinced a judge I was acting contrary to my best interests, and the rest is history."

Maverick's face is unreadable. But I can tell his mind's working.

"Don't you have anything to say?"

He stares out the window, face unmoving. "No. But this changes things, Mia."

"Changes the fact I'm tired of being controlled? So very bone-tired. That I want to decide for myself, just once? To do what's in my best interest. Not what *they* want."

"As guardian, Edwin has—"

36

"I know. I know. Complete control over my finances, my future. But—"

He crosses his arms, shutting down. Not listening. No one listens.

"But—" He waits.

But I can't find the words. Maybe I don't want to. Maybe I still want to think there's someone in this world who would care if they knew my story.

"What does Edwin want?"

Maverick runs a hand over his beard. "Wants to know where you're at. Wants to get you back on tour. Said he could make this easier if you cooperated."

I huff. "Of course."

Silence.

"Money's always the bottom line."

The big cowboy doesn't answer. I shouldn't have expected anything else.

After all, he's my bodyguard, working in an official capacity. His first job. There are lines he won't cross, and can I really blame him?

Or maybe worse, he doesn't care. There's that, too.

I swipe my hand over my cheeks, stopping the tears that want to fall in my coffee.

"We can buy you a few days."

"Thanks," I whisper, staring into the billows of brown and white, like thunderheads in the Nevada heat. "You've already done more than you should have."

"The man at your concert. The one who shot up the place. You sure they have the right guy?"

I shake my head. "Yeah, I got a good look at his face. Countless other witnesses identified him, too."

I scrutinize the world-weary cowboy, but his face gives

no answers. Then, he rises, leaves the room. He returns with a Kleenex box, plopping it down next to me.

I stare at the floral box, disappointment blooming. Of course, he won't help. No one will.

"Sorry I'm so emotional right now."

"Makes sense with all you've been through." His tone is softer now, eyes more perceptive.

"Your parents... Do you know why they hired R&R Security?" Maverick's face is a sudden wall, suspicion shrouded behind his eyes.

"My parents?" I arch my eyebrows. "I have no clue, and honestly, I don't care. They abandoned me long ago. Both of them. Anything they still want from me has to do with money. I can't imagine anything else."

"How can you be so sure?"

My nostrils flare, pulse spiking. "Don't you get it? I'm not sure of anything right now."

He scans the windows, head on a swivel. Always multitasking. "Maybe it had something to do with this concert? This location?"

"Your company's the one they hired. Why not ask Boone about it? I'm sure he knows more than I do."

Maverick frowns, running his hand over his beard.

"Above my pay grade," he says. "According to Boone."

If his mind could make noise, I'd hear gears grinding and pistons firing.

"What?" I ask, fear lodging in my throat for reasons I can't name.

"Nothing," he says, shaking his head and pacing.

I survey the room, a decision brewing. I have to leave this place. Before they bring Edwin here. Before I can't escape again.

I bite my bottom lip, tasting salt and blood. "This morning, I heard you leave early. What were you doing?"

"Securing the perimeter. Making sure you're safe."

"Before dawn? Now, that's dedication."

"Always up that early." He stares at the hands in my lap.

"What will happen? After?"

"After?"

I swallow hard. "Yeah, after ... when Edwin finds out where I'm at."

"Can't tell the future, Princess."

What he doesn't know is that I can. Because the future proves the past. Always has in my case. One unending pattern.

I smile stiffly, pushing the mug away and rising. "I'm going to take a shower."

He nods. "I'll be outside, watching."

It's what I'm counting on.

CHAPTER
SEVEN
MAVERICK

"**D**on't tell me you're one of those hide-with-'em-and-leave-'em girls," I murmur.

Mia startles at my words, jaw dropping, overnight bag clutched guiltily in her hand. I don't know if she's more shocked by my presence or my sudden wordiness.

"I—I—" She stands there awkwardly, eyes round, unmoving.

I step out of the house's afternoon shadow, hands on my hips, dust rising beneath my boots. She went out a window to avoid the front door ... and me.

"Don't let me keep you."

I deliver it slow. Ironic.

She leans back on her heels like I've just slapped her.

Folding my arms over my chest, I narrow my eyes. "See, the thing is, it's easier to protect you if I know where you're at."

Her cheeks flush.

"And this is my first gig. I'd like to keep my job."

Her breath stutters. "I didn't think about that."

I wait, not needing to crowd words into the space between us.

"It's just..." Her eyes drop to the ground. She studies the rust-colored dirt punctuated by bluestem grass like it holds all the answers.

"Mia, talk to me." The words come out more forcefully than I mean them to.

Her expression cracks, anger rushing in. "But I *did* talk to you. Told you about Edwin. The guardianship." Her face is as red as the earth beneath her feet as her voice gains steam. "And you had nothing to say. Like usual."

"Only speak when my words hold power."

She bites her bottom lip, forehead creasing. God, she's beautiful when she's angry—face radiating passion, heat pouring off her body. A force to be reckoned with.

"What are you staring at?" she asks breathlessly.

"You," I answer before my brain has time to catch up. My body's a live wire—awake, hungry.

Stop it, Holt.

"You look at me like you see the real person inside, not the celebrity everyone wants me to be."

I step forward. "Never much cared about fame. It'll break you as easy as it makes you."

"And what do you know about fame?" she asks, tilting up her chin.

I shrug, not ready for this conversation. Not sure I ever will be. I run a hand over my beard, calloused skin scratching across wiry whiskers. "I know it'll catch back up with you ... if you leave now."

"But I can't take this anymore." Her voice quivers, low and raw. "I can call an Uber."

"Can't take what?"

"Can't take being out of control. Helpless. If I don't run now, I may never get this chance again."

"True," I say, slow and easy.

"God, you're frustrating to talk to. Do you know that?"

"Been told that a time or two."

She shifts her feet, raising a cloud of scarlet dust motes that float and linger around her—kissing her blushing skin, dancing over her curves. My throat tightens, body aching, though I order it to stop.

"What if running means they still control you?"

"You know who you remind me of? My therapist. Never saying much of anything, though you still charge by the hour."

I chuckle, surprised by the unexpected observation. "I'm paid to protect. Not provide therapy."

"Well, go on break then. Quit working and talk to me like a fellow human being, not a..." Her mouth twitches as she searches for the word.

"Not a handler?"

"That's it," she says, pointing at me, letting her guard down for one moment.

"Shoot."

Mia drops the bag in the dust. Burgundy clouds snake around her.

"I don't want to feel like a slave in my own life. Like I have no say, no future. Like this tiny respite is asking too much."

I nod, working hard to keep my face unreadable. She needs a punching bag right now. I can be that for her. I widen my stance slightly, waiting for the next verbal blow.

"I don't want to feel like my only value is what I can do for others. How I can make them money. How I can sell my soul, who I am, to keep others financially afloat. No, financially winning." She shakes her head, looking at the toes of her light tan cowboy boots where they touch the hem of her long mint floral sundress. "I don't want to be a cash cow."

"But the guardianship..." I narrow my gaze, taking in her stunning face, the subtle shift in muscles and movements that tells me she's close to breaking down. "That makes everything much trickier."

Her mouth twists for a moment, like she wants to speak but can't find the words. God help me, I can't help but drop my gaze to those plump, pink lips. Let my mind wander off for a moment to how she might taste.

Green eyes snap to mine, and she's caught me. Her cheeks flush again, but not from anger. The corners of her mouth turn up slightly, and a mischievous look captures her face. But her voice comes out steady, pained. "What if a part of me wishes the stalker had done a better job last night?"

Her words knock the air clean out of me.

"Is that wrong of me?" She knits her brow.

Anger burns hot inside, making Nevada midday downright broiling. "Makes those who have made you feel this way wrong, I'd reckon."

"And if you were in my situation, what would you do?"

The question hits closer to home than I'm willing to admit.

Suddenly, a tight laugh escapes her lips. She pinches the bridge of her nose, sinking her head.

"What?"

"It's nothing..."

I wait, shifting uneasily.

"It's just ... for a moment I thought of you singing, dancing, shaking it on stage like I have to..."

"And?" I ask, stuck between a laugh and a grimace.

43

"Well, I can't imagine..." She eyes me for a long moment. "No way."

"You point me in a line, I can dance," I counter too quickly. It's not like I care what she thinks. Not like she should either.

"So, you can dance like you're in *Roadhouse* or something?"

"Something like that," I concede, flexing my jaw.

The air hangs heavy as the heat between us. Can't blame all of it on the sun-baked clay.

"Lemonade? Sweet tea?" I offer, heading toward the front door.

Mia hesitates, eyes sliding over my backside so that when I turn, she's crimson this time. Satisfaction pricks, though I don't care to think about why.

"That limp. Is it an injury, or did you just sleep wrong?" She cocks her head, concern washing across her face. It's beautiful. Like every damn thing about her.

"Maybe I'll tell you about it..."

She quirks her mouth.

"One of these times you tell me I'm off duty."

Then, I slide through the screen door without looking back, trusting she'll follow behind.

EIGHT

MIA

"**Y**ou're off duty," I say halfway through the day. The burly cowboy never misses a beat, sauntering toward the kitchen. Thick thighs, tight ass—denim that's downright criminal.

"Careful," he grunts without turning back around.

"Why?"

He opens the cabinet and pulls out two glasses, filling them with ice from the fridge. "Because, like it or not, you still need a bodyguard—*on duty*."

"Something tells me you never stop protecting."

"Sour or sweet?" he asks, holding up two glass pitchers.

"When life gives you lemons," I trail off, bitterly smiling. Ice clinks against the glass as he pours the liquid, bringing two brimming yellow glasses to the counter.

He pushes one toward me, leaning against the inside of the counter like he needs to keep space between us. That's the last thing on my mind.

He takes a sip and grimaces.

"Maybe more sour than sweet," I say, scrunching my nose at the first swig. "But it hits the spot."

He palms the tiles, face softening. "That comment you said before ... about wishing the stalker did a better job. What did you mean?"

His voice is velvet, the softest I've ever heard it. Anger bristles at the thought he might be patronizing me, but warmth pools in my chest along with a feeling like trust. Dangerous. Misguided. But with Maverick, I can't make myself believe that.

I stare at my glass, watching a bead of sweat roll down the side. Before it hits the counter, I snag it with my finger, bringing the cool droplet to my lips. Maverick's nostrils flare, and his eyes darken as they drop to my mouth. I suck the tip of my finger a second too long, and a low hum escapes his chest. He looks away, gritting his teeth.

No man's ever wanted me for me before. The feeling is liberating. Intimidating. I don't know what I should do with it, though the persistent throb between my legs offers suggestions.

The cowboy swallows hard, eyes narrowing with laser focus on my face. "Answer the question, Mia."

"Are you always this bossy?" I ask, enjoying how his cheeks darken.

"For your well-being? Yeah."

I fish an ice cube from my drink, sucking it slowly between my lips. His gaze follows ... despite himself. The thick veneer of professionalism evaporating. Suddenly, he straightens, fists clenched, turning away.

"You can't avoid this conversation, Princess. Try as you might... to..."

"To?" I drop the cube back in the drink, fluttering my lashes innocently.

"To distract me." Grim-faced, black-voiced.

46

"Distract you?" I laugh throatily. "More like cool off. This place is hotter than hell."

Three long strides, and he's disappeared down the hallway where the thermostat is. Of course. Take things literally.

The hollow thud of boots, and he stands diagonally across from me, arms folded, leaning against the wall. Unaffected. Unreadable. The first man ever to make me rethink my stance against pickup-driving rednecks.

His eyes dart habitually to the windows and doors, still in protection mode.

"Do you ever really stop working?" I ask.

"Not when I have something worth protecting."

I nearly choke on my lemonade, swallowing loudly and gracelessly.

"You are worth it, you know." His face broods—unmoving, eyes storming.

"God, I should never have confessed that to you. Now, I'm never going to hear the end of it." I say it more to berate myself than to engage with him.

"You needed to say it," he says with a finality that sounds like wisdom, though the last thing I want is advice.

I shrug. "Don't make it bigger than it is. It was just a fleeting thought. Not something I'd think about..." I search for the right word, "*regularly*."

"Yeah, but you shouldn't think about it at all."

I huff a sigh, twisting my hands together in front of me. "And I shouldn't be twenty-one with a guardian. But life isn't about what *should* happen, is it?"

"Depends," he rumbles, too dark.

"On what?"

His eyes drop to my mouth again, and heat curls low. My heart hammers against my ribs as I draw the angular planes of his face with my gaze—rough and dangerous. "On whether I'm on or off the clock."

He says it too fast, like he has to force out the words before his brain can catch up. Then, takes a chug of lemonade like a desert-bound man who hasn't drunk in days.

The empty sound of the glass thuds on the counter as he sets it down, refusing to make eye contact. "Just so you know, Mia. Your value isn't in concert tour dates, performance bookings, merch sales. You could give up singing tomorrow, and you'd still be wanted. Needed."

It's like the last part steals something from him, his face hardening. Before I can react, he grabs a sack from the counter, tossing it in my direction. His face says it all. He doesn't trust himself to stay.

"What's this?"

"Nothing," he says, stormy-voiced, heading for the front door. He pauses halfway through, calls over his shoulder without looking back, "Just so we're straight. Next time you decide to leave, ask for a ride. You're no prisoner here."

Then, he disappears. No doubt on one of his perimeter searches. Invisible but never far away.

Plastic rustles as I open the bag. Lavender, mint, and ivory. Three skeins of the softest yarn and a floral tin filled with colorful metal crochet hooks in varying sizes. My fingers slide over the familiar smooth metal, the backs of my eyes stinging dangerously.

"Grandma."

I press the lavender yarn to my face, marveling at its velvety texture. Closing my eyes, I'm transported back to the quiet time between words when gentle hands seamed with wrinkles guided my work and taught me how to craft little turtles and foxes, owls and kittens from string.

But how did he know?

My eyes snap to the door, waiting, breathless, to understand the meaning of this gift and the man behind it. Even more afraid to embody this silence—what I've wanted for so long but don't know how to fill.

"Maverick Holt," I whisper, fingertips glancing over the mint-colored wool. Marveling, unraveling, re-finding myself in the quiet of the room. "You are a mystery."

Warm streams flood my cheeks as it finally hits me all at once. The arena. The stalker. The—

Pop! Pop! Pop!

Playing through my mind, making my body tremble and shake at each remembered sound.

I can still feel the heat of a Nevada night on my skin. Smell the fear. See death—close enough to taste. My shoulders shake with each sob, memories flooding my head. Of the little girl with the crocheted animals. And the woman she became.

No, the brand.

A face that can sell a million copies but not enjoy a single moment of freedom. Do I even know what that means?

On the counter next to me, the phone buzzes, and my spine snaps straight. With shaking hands, I open the screen. One missed call and a fresh string of texts from Edwin.

> This is exactly why the guardianship exists.
>
> You're clearly not well.
>
> Have you stopped taking your medication?

Maybe he's right. Maybe I can't do this on my own.

Maybe I'm being stupid or selfish or spiraling into another psychiatric episode.

Or maybe ... just for once, I'm taking accountability for myself. Making my own choices. Choosing my own path.

As scary as the last thought is, it breaks something loose that bound me for as long as I can remember. With trembling hands, I go into Edwin's contact information and block him.

Done.

Over.

For a few moments, I stare at the white tile kitchen countertop. It stares back, a blank slate. Like my future.

What do I feel? I catalog my senses. The ache in my throat, the sting in my eyes. The pumping of my heart and fast-paced breaths. Fear, excitement, anxiety. I feel them all at once, like some great wave of emotion.

But what I don't feel? Loss, grief, impending insanity.

I may not know what comes next. But one thing is true. I feel no regret about letting go of Edwin... and fame. And the career I never wanted.

Admitting it feels like a sin. Embracing it, a foreign country. And yet I know, for change to happen, it must start with me.

CHAPTER

NINE

MAVERICK

I hold the phone to my ear, pacing a little way from the cabin. Still close enough to protect—but far enough to give Mia the space and time she needs.

"Did I do okay?" Jack asks.

"Yes, thanks."

"Never shopped for that stuff before. Had to ask for help."

I chuckle, imagining the gruff, ex-military cowboy awkwardly casing the crafts section at the grocery store for Mia's gift.

Mia's gift.

What the hell am I doing? But the woman needs something to do with her hands. And maybe I need to give her back a piece of herself. No matter how small.

It's what I'd want.

A nauseating flutter grips my stomach. Dust, blood, the roar of the crowd. Fifteen hundred pounds of muscle coming down hard, pressing me into the grit of the arena. More than tendons wrecked, muscles smashed. A whole life shattered. Another me now relegated to shadow.

"Mav? You still there?"

Stop thinking, Holt. Stop feeling.

"Yeah."

"Like I said. You let me know when you're ready for a break, and I'll take over. Pretty damn quiet here since the debrief."

I joined the meeting on my phone. Learned more than I care to think about.

"That Edwin guy's a piece of work..."

I grunt. Already courtesy called the Ranch, demanding Mia's return. Said the matter could be resolved without the courts ... *if* we turn her back over. But Boone won't budge.

I don't want to think about what this could cost.

"Makes you wonder who she needs saving from."

He laughs, tense and forced. "You just said the quiet part out loud."

Not my place. Probably. But maybe I don't care.

"Boone won't cave to that kind of shit."

"Figured as much," I say, "but he probably should. Don't like the thought of R&R Security going up against music moguls over all of this."

"You mean, over one pretty lady."

I exhale. "One asset."

He chuckles. Deep voices rumble in the background, and Jack says something. "Got to go."

I shouldn't have asked him to get the gift. Now, I'll never hear the end of it.

But it's worth every risk—the fear of looking unprofessional. The threat of rumors about the girl. When I enter the cabin, I find her on the couch, singing and hooking fuzzy strips of fiber into a small circle.

I cock my head, taking in the scene. The beauty frowns with concentration, graceful fingers flying. No longer performing. No longer playing a part. It puts an ache behind my ribs.

Lavender and blueberry waft toward me from the big ceramic mug beside her. The tisane's fragrance twists and twirls with her perfume—all plums, roses, and *need*.

Twenty-one. Too young for a thirty-five-year-old retired bull rider. She's got her whole life ahead of her. Mine's already in the rearview.

"Thought it would be harder. That I wouldn't remember how, but my fingers knew." She looks up, a fragile smile greeting me. "For the life of me, I can't figure something out, though."

"And what's that?" I ask, hanging my hat on the hook by the door and stabbing my fingers through the hair plastered to my forehead. Still hotter than hell out there.

"How you found the time to get this?"

I shrug. "Colleague owed me a favor."

Her lips press into a firm line, eyes going misty. "And how ... you *knew?*"

"You needed something in your hands. Something sturdy. Something grounding. Then, while researching your case, I came across an old *Good Morning USA* clip."

Her mint eyes dance over my face, soft, intentional, like a caress.

"No matter how you come across, Maverick, you actually *do* care."

I shift uneasily. Words almost stumble out, but I won't let them. She doesn't need an asshole. And she doesn't need a liar. Instead, I say, "Yes, I *do* care ... about you."

Her eyes drop to her hands, her face darkening. "Makes me wonder..."

"Wonder what?"

"How different things could be if I were just a woman, and you were just a man—not my bodyguard?"

My chest tightens, a sharp ache lodging behind my ribs.

"Stuff like that. What-ifs will make you mighty crazy."

She sets the yarn and crochet hook in her lap. "What-ifs are the only thing that keep me going."

"I don't get it," I confess, stepping closer and eyeing the spot next to her on the couch. Can't go there. Won't let myself. "You've got everything people dream of," I murmur. "And it still isn't enough?"

"What I have, *I* never wanted."

Questions snake through my mind. But only one matters. "Then what are you going to do about it?"

She pats the spot next to her. "I won't bite, and—"

"I know. I know. I'm off duty," I say impatiently, taking the seat opposite her in front of the hearth. "Only I'm not, Mia."

"What you *are* is no fun at all," she says decidedly, corners of her mouth drawing down until I'm pretty sure she's pouting.

Never had a woman accuse me of this before. Not since the injury stole my dream.

"Not here for fun. Here to protect."

Her face goes imperious. "Then, you might as well make yourself useful. How about refilling the kettle and heating more water for me? My tea could use a refresh."

I give her a warning glare, not amused by the sudden shift into servitude. "Anything else, Princess?"

Her face goes mischievous again, and I brace for more temptation. "Just honey. Lots of honey."

Fuck. She has to go there. My fists ball, and I mutter under my breath. Last complication I need—wanting my asset. One so high-profile, there's no way I'll avoid scrutiny.

When I place two steaming mugs on the table, she pats the spot next to her on the couch again. "Remember when I said I wanted a human to talk to?"

I nod.

Sarcasm threads her laugh. "Guess I'll have to make do with you."

"Let me guess," I grumble.

"Off duty," she says with a look that tells me exactly why that's a problem.

CHAPTER
TEN
MIA

"Off duty," Maverick says like a man unconvinced by his own words. He begrudgingly sits down next to me.

"You couldn't look less thrilled if you tried," I murmur, snuggling back against his shoulder, returning to my crocheting. He stiffens, holding his breath, but he doesn't pull away. "Need I remind you, people pay thousands of dollars just to meet and snap a selfie with me?"

"Doesn't make any of this right."

I chuckle. "Maverick Holt. The newbie. The man who puts duty above all else. The man who gives gifts he maybe shouldn't."

He clears his throat, face tight. "That a threat?"

"No, just an observation. An acknowledgment that there's more to you than you're willing to let on."

"Maybe." His face looks torn.

"Never sat like this with a man before," I confess—*this close, this quiet.*

He balks, eyes zinging electricity.

56

"I somehow have trouble believing that, Ms. Love. But if you're feeling uncomfortable—"

He starts to rise. But I reach out, resting a hand on his muscular shoulder. "Please. Not yet. You make me feel safe. Safer than anybody ever has."

He shifts away, but not so far that we stop touching. "That's exactly why this shouldn't be happening. I'm not here to take advantage of you."

"You've made that abundantly clear." My voice sounds raw, and my eyes sting again. "I'd ask for a hug, but something tells me you wouldn't give it."

"No."

Cold. Resolved.

"So, I'll take what you *can* give me. Off the clock, of course."

His hands fist, and his face tightens. "I don't know what you're getting at, but—"

"Nothing. Absolutely nothing. I swear."

His sigh comes out like a low hum, brows furrowing, eyes trying to read me.

"I need to feel safe. Just for a moment."

"But I'm sweaty and hot. Probably smell terrible."

"Your smell? That's what you're worried about?" I ask with a giggle.

"No," he answers morosely, looking away. "I'm worried about my job. My future. Crossing a line I shouldn't."

The words take more from him than he's willing to admit. His honesty, his vulnerability, make me want him even more. His shoulder is firm against my back, steady, like it could anchor me through any storm. My mind devolves, wondering what the rest of him would feel like against me.

"Just for the record, you smell like pine sap and something else ... something darker, very masculine."

He crosses his arms, grimacing. "Glad my deodorant's to your liking."

I snort. "If that's what it is, then, yes."

He inhales sharply. "We about done here?"

The words sting like rejection. But his eyes burn with something he won't name, body stiff with restraint, not disinterest.

"Almost," I say, smiling at the flare of his nostrils, the hunger in his gaze. I loop the soft wool around the hook, pulling it through for another dainty stitch. "Just thinking about another life and different circumstances. Maybe a man who's not a bodyguard and a woman who's free to choose. They have a farm together somewhere. Land stretches in all directions as far as the eye can see. Maybe toward snow-capped mountains on one side, an ancient fence line on another..."

"A creek on the other," he adds, face brooding. "And a forest."

"Yes," I say wistfully, closing my eyes for a moment, picturing it in my mind. "The woman has a wool shop. Rows upon rows of soft skeins, dyed in muted tones. Organic hues, because, you know..."

A grandfather clock ticks from the corner, the air conditioner firing back up with a lazy wheeze.

"So, maybe they have sheep?" he asks, concentrating on the empty hearth. Pity it's summer. I can almost imagine the firelight dancing in those dark eyes.

"Maybe. Or how about Angora bunnies?"

"Bunnies? Seriously, woman? Next, you'll be saying llamas ... or alpacas—"

"Yes!" I set the crocheting down, clapping my hands together. "Alpacas are it."

He shifts stiffly but doesn't move away. Not one inch, though the heat between us boils. Climate control or not.

He quirks his mouth deep in thought. "A far cry from the stage and fame..."

"Far as you can get, I'd imagine."

He eyes me, able to hide every emotion, though I can tell his thoughts are rolling again—with the force of a freight train. "That really what you want? Peace? Quiet?"

"With the right person, I think so."

The air sizzles between us, thick enough to cut.

Without warning, he explodes to his feet, pacing toward the hearth and resting his hands on the mantle. "You'd like it for a few days, maybe weeks. But then you'd miss it."

"Miss what?"

"The roar of the crowd. The fame. The people stomping their feet and chanting your name. Nothing like it in the world. It could haunt a person."

He says it as if he understands. Like he's speaking from experience rather than wisdom.

"Is that what you miss?" I ask.

He turns to face me, a dizzy sort of pain written in his features. And with it, anger. The realization hits me too late. I've asked something unforgivable.

Maverick slides past me slow and easily. But his face can't hide the storm. "Back on duty. Permanently, just so we're clear."

His words are a slamming door.

"But—"

"Need to make some phone calls."

I follow him with my eyes, breath hitching. I pushed too

far. Now, I'm going to pay for it. Should've known better. Never met a person with steeper, thicker walls except for me. "You're not leaving me. Are you?"

"Not yet."

"But soon?" I knit my brow.

"We could both use a shift change."

"Maybe you can take a break," I reply, voice shaking. "But this is my life, and as far as I can tell, you're the only person on this planet who I can trust right now. Please don't forget it."

He opens his mouth to lie to me. Maybe to tell me I'm wrong, or I've got other options. But then, our eyes meet, and he clenches his jaw. "I won't forget."

I can tell by the steel in his voice, the intensity in his gaze, that he means what he says. More than anyone ever has before. And so I don't say goodbye. Because this doesn't feel like an ending.

ELEVEN

MAVERICK

A day and a half since I last saw Mia. It doesn't mean I've stopped thinking about her... or her situation. About the manager whose pathological need for control keeps tightening.

I glance at my watch, wiping the sweat from my forehead. Eight-minute mile. Still not as long as eight seconds used to feel.

Dawn's golden fingers peek through the dark sky, heat following close behind. Would rather be out riding this morning. But I need to hurt. To grind down the physical, to set hard boundaries that can't be crossed.

Back at headquarters, where Boone offered to let me crash, I shower in silence.

Steam clouds the glass, the sound of water a steady roar, but it does nothing to quiet my head. Or my body. I turn the faucet to cold and wait.

Mia is there anyway.

Golden curls brush her shoulders. The faintest hint of plum and roses—clean, soft, unmistakable. Her mouth, full and expressive, the kind that looks like it tells the truth even when she doesn't mean to. Those green eyes that never quite stop watching, even when she's trying to disappear.

I brace my hands against the tile, letting the cold water run down my back. My jaw tightens. My chest feels too full, like there's no room left to breathe without giving something away.

I shouldn't want this... shouldn't want her. But *want* doesn't ask permission.

Heat coils low, sharp and unwelcome, a reminder that my body hasn't gotten the memo about restraint or rules or consequences. I lean my forehead against the glass and close my eyes, breathing through it, refusing to move my hands, refusing the easy out.

I don't take the edge off. I don't reach for anything but control. Because wanting her like this—unfinished, unanswered—is the point. Anything else would be a lie. A way to pretend I can have part of her without choosing all of her.

The water turns cold. I welcome the bite. Let it burn. Let it remind me where the line is.

Still, her face lingers. The way she leaned back against me earlier, trusting without asking. The weight of that trust settles heavy in my chest.

I straighten, shut off the water, and grab a towel.

This doesn't end here. It can't.

Between swigs of black coffee, I do a background check on Edwin. No arrests. No record. Mia Love's manager for eight years.

Then, I search her name again, heart pumping as I type out the letters. I find her real name—Mia Lowell. Then, her parents. Divorced when she was ten.

Father's name: Justin Lowell.

A Southern businessman. Owns his own private jet service with ties to just about every big-money industry in the country. Wouldn't be a stretch to think he needs occasional security assistance. Or that R&R steps in.

"Justin Lowell," I say out loud, curiosity and guilt fighting for dominance.

I shouldn't be doing this, researching an asset's associates. But I keep going anyway.

Mia's face flashes in my mind—the way she looked at me when she confessed I'm the only person she trusts. It stoked the one need I can't deny—to protect her at all costs. Which means the one thing I can't admit out loud.

She's no longer an asset. She's someone I would cross lines for, and if it comes to it, I will choose her.

That terrifies me.

Because it changes everything. Just like news of her guardianship. Not sure I'm ready for those stakes.

But I am certain I can't turn them down.

Mia needs faith in humanity again—peace, safety, something real. I can't be the one who denies her that. Though it could cost me everything.

I take another swig of coffee. A little too hot, burning on the way down. Not as sizzling as that sliver of touch when she leaned back against me, and we talked about stuff that could get me fired.

"Can't let that happen, Holt. Can't let Boone down." I speak the words into silence, appraising the minimally furnished compound bedroom.

Ex-military, ex-rodeo. I've always lived by pain and blood ... and the ethic that comes with them.

But with Mia, nothing's that simple. And that's why I keep typing, and I keep researching until it's time to report for our morning briefing.

I STARE at the stack of papers on Boone's desk, the clock ticking in the background. Counting down what we're almost out of—time.

"A cease-and-desist. Crowe wants her back, and he's no longer playing."

"What does *that* mean?" Jack asks in low tones next to me.

"He's threatening to have her declared noncompliant ... demanding an institutional review."

I clench my jaw, shoulders tightening.

"He's talking medications, involuntary return ... it's pretty much all on the table at this point."

Jack crosses his arms, sits back, and shakes his head.

"How much time?" I ask.

"Forty-eight hours, though the lawyers think we can maybe buy her a week."

And then, she'll disappear again. Maybe this time, forever.

I can't let that happen.

"Anything we can do about it?" I cough, correcting myself quickly. "I mean, her parents can do?"

Boone shifts uneasily. "Maybe. If she'd open up to someone. Trust them with what's really going on."

A warning bell sounds in my head.

"That what this is all about?" I ask, like he and I are the only two men in the room, like chairs aren't congregated around his desk in a half-moon, rapt faces listening.

Boone's eyes narrow. "What are you getting at, Holt?"

I eye him silently. Doesn't take words for him to know.

He turns to Jack. "How'd it go?"

"Fine."

"She say anything to you?"

He shrugs. "Not a word she didn't have to. Made it clear Mav's the only one she'll talk to."

Jack eyes me with a chuckle. "Not sure what you did, but you're all she wants."

"For God's sake," I grumble, trying to mask the heat that climbs my neck.

"Hmm," our boss says. The leather of his chair creaks as he leans back, staring at the ceiling.

"How do we help her?" I hear myself ask, like I'm outside of my body. No longer in control of myself. Dammit. I need more space from this case.

Not to care. Not to make it so damn obvious.

"The question on everyone's mind." Boone frowns. "No easy answer."

The room goes silent for a long, untenable moment.

"Holt, you're back with Mia."

What? But I know better than to question a superior, especially in front of the rest of the crew.

"Need to use what little time we have strategically. She's told you more than anybody else, and it's clear she trusts you. So, keep us posted on everything."

I nod, clench my jaw, and stare at the floor for one moment. May live to regret this.

"Sir," I say, leveling my gaze at him, "mind if we have a word alone?"

Boone leans forward, face uncompromising. Then, his eyes dart past me. "You heard the newbie. Back to work, everyone. Be there shortly."

After the shuffling of chairs and footfalls settles, and the door closes behind us, I face Boone, body tense. Not quite sure what to say or how much to give away.

He rests his arms on the desk, hands folded, waiting.

"You said it yourself, Sir. Mia trusts me, which means I

need to know—with certainty—that what I'm doing is for the right reasons." I pause for a moment, then add, "In her best interests." I have to say this because no one else will.

"Rest assured, this is for Mia."

"Not the pop star. The woman."

His eyes narrow. Then, he nods curtly. "Report back everything. Understood?"

"Understood," I grunt.

I've spent my life believing there is always a right and a wrong way. Hell, it's how I succeeded in the National Guard and the rodeo ring.

But now, there's only this... Protect her. Or protect the rules that failed her. I don't have to think twice about what I'll do.

CHAPTER

TWELVE

MIA

I see him from a distance, sauntering toward me.

Ebony hair glistening blue in the sunlight. Square-cut jaw and chiseled face. Gait wary, with a slight limp. Eyes black as a starless sky.

My breath catches in my throat as I walk the clothesline, singing and pinning up white sheets and towels. They flutter in the breeze like ghosts, billowing, unfurling, hiding, and then revealing him to me over and over as he draws closer.

My chest aches, eyes dangerously stinging. Why do I always want the one thing I can't have? The one person not interested?

But my body won't listen. A wide grin seizes my face as he draws near, heat radiating from my cheeks. He puts his hands on his hips, staring too long. Like he's recognizing something that was always there.

"Ms. Love."

"Holt."

His eyes narrow, jaw tightening. "Dryer broken?"

I shake my head. "Wanted to do something the old-fashioned way for once." *The way that makes it feel worthwhile.*

He nods, brows furrowing. "You okay?"

"Fine."

He hesitates, mouth working. But nothing comes out. I return to my clothespins and line, humming softly to myself.

Grandma speaks through the whispers of the wind-rustled fabric. Like she talks to me through the yarn and crochet hook. The only person who wanted *me*—not Mia Love.

Warmth may lurk behind Maverick's eyes, but he's no different from everyone else. I'm a means to an end for him. To secure his job. To satisfy his need for responsibility, hard work, whatever.

"Can I help you?" He removes his Stetson, wiping the back of his arm over his forehead.

"No, thank you."

His face goes stony, body stiff and straight. Wheeling around, he strides away.

Only then, with his back turned to me, do I ask, "What's the plan for me?"

He stops, head dropping, though he never looks back.

I add, "I know about the cease-and-desist." I swallow loudly. "Edwin contacted me, too."

"And what did he say?"

I shrug, though he never looks back. "He talked about contracts, the guardianship ... what will happen if I don't go back on my meds." I laugh bitterly. "Concerns about my well-being. All very reasonable, even altruistic."

"Sounds like what happens next is up to you," he murmurs.

I snort. "Sounds like the opposite of that to me."

"What do you want, Mia?"

Already told you, but you didn't listen.

The sting of rejection from earlier still lingers. I'm not used to that ... or wanting a different outcome.

"I want time," I whisper. "Quiet. A moment to breathe."

He nods, eyes straining to the distant horizon. "We're trying to buy you that. But we need more information. A better understanding of what this all is."

I freeze, the last glimmer of hope about Maverick evaporating. He's not here because he wants to be. He's here because it's another job. My trusting him hasn't been connection. It's been transactional all along. Like every other aspect of my life.

That's when I know I have to do this alone.

A thousand questions fill my head. Is that why my parents hired R&R Security? Is that why they let me choose Maverick? Because they're trying to help me, like Edwin? Or is it about what everyone wants—a money maker?

My voice trembles. "I imagine you've seen the papers yourself. Edwin said R&R got served."

Maverick nods, wheeling back around. His eyes are dark, dangerous.

"Edwin promised to make things easier if you go back now," he says flatly. "That's his word. Not mine."

I step back, absorbing the hard sting of his words. I knew Maverick was all business. But I never thought he'd offer the same temptation as my manager.

"Easier isn't easy."

He steps closer, forehead creases deepening. I could almost read his face as concern. But I can't make that mistake. "Easy isn't what you want, anyway."

I look down at the wicker hamper filled with freshly washed linens. *Doesn't matter what I want. No need to waste my breath saying it, though. If he hasn't figured it out yet, he never will.*

I raise my chin, eyeing him coolly. "I'll be in shortly."

He stops, mouth working. I almost think he has more to say, but nothing comes out.

Turning back to the laundry, I grab another piece, pinning it up.

"Gonna do a perimeter sweep. Be back shortly."

I nod without answering.

THE WHITE TILE of the kitchen countertop glares at me, cool and uncaring. Burnt orange and white bottles line the counter in neat rows. The instructions echo the pattern of my life.

Take with food before bedtime. Take on an empty stomach. Three per day when symptoms persist. May cause drowsiness, depression, apathy.

Actually, it's my life causing these things.

The phone is beside me again. Edwin is using a different number to communicate with me. He assures me he'll keep using new lines until I realize blocking him won't change a thing.

I pop a child-proof cap, shuffle a few white pills into the palm of my hand. Take enough, and I won't care anymore. Take more, and it won't matter.

You can be a zombie as long as you don't wake up. Edwin knows this well. That's why the prescription regimen started young. Along with the gaslighting, the manipulation, the abuse that made me second-guess myself.

But going back to that life now? Not possible.

Maverick stands in the hallway, half shrouded in shadow, observing me. Face watchful and clouded, features rougher and more rugged than I've ever seen him.

My eyes flicker to his, absorbing the warmth he can't hide, hating the restraint that hangs like a paper-thin shield between us.

"Edwin says I'm crazy. That I would implode my life without him."

The black-haired cowboy shifts uneasily, folding his arms over his broad chest.

"But there's not enough here to control me anymore." I rub a hand over my face, exhaling loudly. "Don't worry, though," I say low and raw. "I have a plan."

"And what's that?" he grumbles, face hard as granite.

"Does it matter to you?"

Pain slashes through his face for an instant. Then, a stony resolve. I could almost think I imagined it. But I know better.

"What do you do when you need something from the store?" I ask.

He straightens, jaw ticking. "I get it."

I nod. "Easy. Simple. But if I go out in public? It's a madhouse. Paparazzi everywhere. Journalists scrutinizing me. Tabloids jonesing for the worst angle of me. The moment of disgust, the bad outfit, the unfiltered sentence that they can use against me over and over again."

"And Edwin?" His voice sounds softer, but I can't mistake it for care.

"Edwin protects me. Edwin cares for me. Edwin keeps me sane and safe and..." My eyes drop back to the line of bottles. "Medicated."

"With all due respect..." he drawls.

I arch an eyebrow waiting.

"He'll use you until you have nothing left to give. He'll take and take and take. Your fame, your talent, your beauty, your youth ... until you become exactly what he's trying to make you."

"And what's that?"

"Disposable."

He doesn't say the last part like some abstract hypothetical. He says it like a man who knows the sting of losing it all.

"People like you have spent their whole lives learning how to be. People like me inhabit glass cages." My voice quivers at the end.

"You could figure it out if people would let you."

"And I will figure it out," I answer too quickly. "Alone."

With a sweep of my arm, I send the medications cascading into the trash bin beside the counter. Plastic bites the air. Pills strike hollow and final.

Maverick's face stills, his eyes brooding. They slide past me to the window. Another sweep of the room, like assassins will jump out of the cracks in the floors if he doesn't keep watch.

"Laundry's dry. I'll help."

I open my mouth to refuse the offer, but the determination in his walk tells me to save my breath.

THIRTEEN

MAVERICK

B oone's voice seethes with resignation. "The lawyers her parents hired aren't optimistic. If we could just get more time..."

I stand a distance away watching the blonde beauty pull fabric from the line, white cloth billowing around her like a lacy veil.

"Is she confiding in you? Giving us anything we can work with?" he asks, steely-voiced.

"Getting there, though nothing solid yet."

"I see," he says as if he doesn't quite believe me.

He shouldn't. Mia's gone cold, silent. Achingly polite.

She's not punishing me for anything I did. She's learning to live with the decision I made.

For both of us.

The kind of decision you make before the roar of the crowd dies down—and you realize she's still standing there alone.

I rub my hand over my beard. "What does the attorney need?"

Boone lets out a low sigh. "Ideally, proof of abuse, coercion, forced medication, or a credible third-party witness."

"Shouldn't the lawyers talk to her directly?"

"The way the law reads, she needs a judge to sign off on legal counsel."

"Are you serious?" I grimace. "She sounds like a slave."

"But does *she* think she is? That's what matters. That's what I need you to sort out."

"Okay," I murmur, though I already know it's too late. What happened when I walked out the other day. When I turned my back on her at her most vulnerable moment... I'm not sure it can be repaired.

I thought it was restraint. The right thing to do. But as her frigid voice, terse demeanor, and far-off gaze attest, everything has changed.

I should tell Boone this, admit where I went wrong. But restraint was easier than choosing her.

Yet, despite everything, something about Mia won't let me walk away. Even if she's already left me far behind.

Inside the cabin, she sits at the counter, typing into her laptop. A Word document is pulled up, and her fingers fly.

"You take up writing since the last time I was here?"

Her mouth is a frown of concentration. She doesn't answer, face cold and composed. I feel some of her ice lodge in the warm spot where my heart should be.

"So, I get the silent treatment now?"

Her fingers freeze, mint eyes snapping to my face. "What?" She asks too innocently, like we're strangers.

"You heard me."

She shrugs, eyes gliding back to the screen. "Didn't think you wanted to talk anymore. On duty permanently, remember?"

I snort, ready to eat my own words. My restraint has

taught her not to rely on me. My seeming indifference transformed her need into distance. I hate myself for it.

"Mia..."

"What?" God, she wears indifference cold.

"The not talking to me. The medication. The typing. What are you planning?" I put my hands on my hips, forehead creasing.

"Does it matter to you?"

"You know me better than that."

Her eyes narrow, fire glinting behind the cool green. "I know you want to keep things professional. I'm helping you now."

"Professional doesn't mean silence ... or putting up walls," I counter, annoyed by how helpless this conversation makes me feel.

"If you must know," she says, closing the laptop and spinning around toward me on the stool. "I've kept a journal for years now. It's where I detail stuff. Write down what's happening, what's being done for me."

I cross my arms. "And what's being done *to* you?"

"Either you already know, and you're asking to gain my trust. Or you're the clueless newbie who can't help me, anyway."

I shift back on my heels, swallowing loudly. "What if it's something else?"

She chuckles, shaking her head. "No offense. But it never is."

"What if I do want to earn your trust, but not for the reasons you think?" I ask gruffly.

"You already lost it," she says pointedly, like what's done is done. Forever.

"I get where you're going with this. That I maybe didn't handle things right before. But this isn't about me. It's about you and your manager and what you want your life to look like."

"What I want my life to look like? Now, that's rich!" She stands, pacing back and forth, hand going to her mouth deep in thought. "I'm forced to take medication I don't need. I'm treated like a child without the ability to function or make my own decisions. Hell, I'm a virgin, and yet I still have an IUD, just in case. Just to make sure nothing—not romance, not family, not a future—gets in the way of Edwin's plans for me."

I inhale sharply, stung by her words and knocked flat by the pain etched on her face. "See, that's what we need to know, Mia. So your parents can help you."

"My parents?" She screams, raising her hands. "Are you out of your mind? Who do you think signed away parental rights to Edwin in the first place? God, this is pointless!"

"And so what are you going to do, Mia?" I ask darkly.

She stops pacing, eyes drilling into me. Like she's searching for a connection she can no longer find.

"I'm going to... I'm going to get a lawyer, and I'm going to make a huge legal stink, and—"

"The guardianship blocks you from seeking legal counsel unless it's court-appointed."

She bites her bottom lip, face going as white as the sheets on the line earlier.

"But you already know that, don't you?"

Her head sinks back, and she lets out a ragged sigh. "I have a plan now. One where I don't need help. Not from you. Not from anyone else. I'm going to appeal directly to my fans. Try to put enough public pressure on the legal system, on Edwin, on whoever will listen so that I can finally be free."

"I know you don't want to believe this, Mia, but I can help."

A caustic laugh escapes her lips. "You?" She arches an eyebrow, imperious like the princess I once took her for. "You'd have to care to be able to help me. So would R&R Security. So would my parents. But if there's anything I've learned from this situation, it's this: I can't rely on anyone."

What scares me most about her words isn't that she rages or makes a loud scene. It's the way her gestures diminish, her voice goes quiet, as she speaks with the kind of determination that means I can't change her mind.

Turns out, the most fragile thing about Mia Love was never her safety or her ego. It wasn't the public persona or the fame. It was the trust she placed in me—the trust I shattered without a word or a second glance.

CHAPTER

FOURTEEN

MIA

Before Maverick can answer, I grab my laptop, heading silently for the bedroom.

"Is that it?" he asks, raw-voiced, face darkening.

I let the click of the closed door answer for me. An ache tugs at my ribs. Maybe I'm being too hard on him. But I can't fall back into old patterns. Like waiting for someone to save me. If there's anything Maverick has taught me, it's that I ultimately must act alone.

Hours pass in a flash, the only witness shadows creeping long across the floor as I hit the record button again. Try to get it right.

Nothing about this is performance. It's raw. Authentic. Dangerous. Yet, my body trembles, and a knot tightens in my stomach. Am I walking into another Edwin trap without even knowing it?

As sunset turns the Nevada sky wild—a brazen glow in horizontal stripes of blue, gold, and rose—I pad back out into the living room, sitting cross-legged on the couch.

Maverick stands by the window, body tense, eyes trained on the edge of the property. Vigilant, steady.

"You want to talk about it?" he asks without moving a muscle.

"On the record or off the record?" Anger surges inside. Am I really ready to make the same mistake all over again with him? The mistake that could cost me any chance at freedom?

He turns, dark eyes washing over me, brows furrowed. "Off-duty and off the record." He grits out the words, like they cost him something.

I hesitate for a moment, questions flitting through my mind like dandelion fuzz in the wind. But I can tell he's past reflection, his face sheer determination. Whether or not he wants to, whether it's right or wrong, I know he'll help me.

I take a deep breath, lick my lips. His eyes drop to my mouth, and the room sizzles. "I made a video," I say, trying to keep my voice steady. "An appeal to my fans for help."

He nods, jaw tense.

"What, no trying to talk me out of it?" I raise an eyebrow.

"I'm here to support you first, Mia. Protect you second and give advice only if you ask for it."

No one's ever trusted me so much. My throat tightens, a dangerous sting gathering behind my eyes.

"Okay," I say, and it feels like two syllables lay me bare before my bodyguard. "Tell me what you think."

Without hesitation, he crosses the room, carefully taking a seat next to me. Too close to be professional, but still navigating a careful line. I hand him my laptop, and he watches twice, face unreadable, mouth unmoving.

"What do you think?" I ask when I can't take the suspense anymore.

"Tell me what you want me to comment on." His voice is warm but guarded.

"If it's believable. If I make sense. If I should post it."

His eyes wander to mine, face torn. "I can't tell you what you should or shouldn't do. But I *can* give my opinion on the other two factors, for what it's worth."

For what it's worth. Far more than you may ever realize.

He exhales slowly. "Believable? Yes. Clear and logical? Completely."

"But?"

"But I can't shake the feeling Edwin will find a way to use this against you."

My stomach drops. Not because he's telling me anything I don't already know, but because he had the courage to be honest. It could cost him, and he knows it.

"Okay. Then what else do I do?"

The room goes silent. He stares ahead, expression storming. "I faced something similar once. A contract I shouldn't have been let out of. Only fate stepped in, handling it for me. In your case, though, I don't feel Edwin will ever voluntarily let go."

"Agreed." I want to probe deeper, find out what he means by a contract and fate. But that's not the conversation we need to have right now.

"You have to find a way to let the public know something is wrong without triggering immediate legal retaliation."

"Easier said than done," I huff.

"The risk you've awakened a sleeping bear will always be there. But you could minimize it by being more factual, more restrained. By appealing to logic and reason rather than emotion."

I let the words—and the fact this man is helping me—sink in.

"No accusations yet, just mention of a pattern."

"Yes," I whisper, drawing a little closer to him, though I know I shouldn't. I need to feel Maverick's presence as much as I perceive it. He doesn't move away or betray concern, even when our thighs touch on the couch.

"I think you should use your real name, too," he says, and the weight of what we're discussing finally sinks in. This could blow up my whole life. End my career. Especially if Edwin has his way ... and he *always* does.

"When I start talking, I trigger the fallout—whether immediate or more measured. I know that much."

"The woman I'm looking at is strong enough to handle it," he says calmly.

"You have more faith in me than I do," I confess with a soft laugh. "I've spent most of my life being told what was best for me, which means I'm still learning—slowly—that silence doesn't equal stability."

"No, it doesn't. But words for words' sake, emotion for drama won't help you either. You need cold, calculated fact. That's what Edwin fears most, I'd imagine."

"So maybe a written statement then. Something that will make my fans notice. That might get advocacy groups involved."

He nods, face stern without being mean. "Something that makes Edwin's response look like guilt rather than a curtain he can hide behind."

MORE HOURS PASS as I pore over years of journals—

81

documenting abuse, framing timelines, ordering and aligning facts—until the truth is impossible to ignore.

Maverick sets a fresh mug of tea down on the coffee table, eyes dark and warm, as I read back through my statement again, mouth moving wordlessly.

To see my life laid out without emotion, detailed with quiet precision, knowing that what I allude to is only a tiny sliver of what I've endured... It's almost too much. It feels dangerous, far more dangerous than my earlier candid attempts at videos.

I let out a sigh that carries weight, weight I didn't know I'd been holding this whole time.

"What can I do?" he asks quietly, the friend I need instead of the bodyguard I require.

I stare into my mug for a long moment, measuring the cost of what I'm compelled to ask. This will change everything between us.

I bite my bottom lip until I taste salt and metal, hands fidgeting.

He turns away, strides to the kitchen counter, and returns with a crochet hook and yarn. He sets them on the arm next to me wordlessly.

"Sorry, it's not alpaca yarn. I'll do better next time."

His words are the peace offering I need. The corners of my mouth turn up despite myself, and his face lightens subtly.

"Will you read this for me now? Give me your honest opinion?"

"Of course, Mia. But I'm no lawyer, and I don't understand the intricacies of all of this. So, take what I have to say with a grain of salt."

"I know." I sigh, fingering the soft wool with one hand, letting its feel transport me back to another time and place.

"But I still trust you more than anyone on the face of this earth."

The words make me feel smaller, like I'm back on the soundstage to *Good Morning USA*, waiting for Edwin to snatch my stuffed animal friends.

"Then, I won't break that trust again, Mia Lowell. No matter what it costs me." Something shifts in his face—not softness, not relief.

Resolve. The kind that only comes when a man knows he's crossed a line he can never uncross.

He says my name as if he's seeing me for the first time. Truly seeing me, and I can't doubt his words. They crack open something in my heart that I didn't even know was there, and my mind wanders to a future I'll never have. And the man who can't be anything more than my temporary bodyguard.

Sitting next to me, he reads through it several times without saying a thing. Finally, his eyes meet mine over the laptop screen, all pupil so that they're two ebony orbs.

"Is there anything that would make it easier for them to say I'm crazy?" I ask.

Maverick pushes the laptop back toward me, drawing closer. He doesn't stop until I feel the heat of his body on my arm and shoulder, with only a thin sliver of air between us. Safety, ache, and need all at once.

My throat thickens, heart pounding against my ribs. I remember the feel of his arms like steel bands around me. God, I need them again.

He points to a line on the screen. "That adverb. It could be spun, I think."

I cut it, staring at him.

His face storms, nostrils flaring. Air escapes my lips, his eyes filled with a hungry desire I haven't seen since his return. "Wait six hours before posting, at a bare minimum."

"Tomorrow, then. After I sleep on everything."

Silence stretches long between us; no need to speak. Touching with our eyes. Somehow it feels more intimate than flesh ever could.

"Want to take your tea outside? Sit beneath the stars?" he asks, and it feels like starting over. Something I'd given up hoping would happen between us.

"Only if you hold me," I whisper.

His mouth twitches. "That what you need?"

"Yes, it's what I need." The words make me feel naked in front of him.

"Alright then," he says, offering his hand.

FIFTEEN

MAVERICK

"This porch needs a swing," I say, seated on the top step, a swirl of plum-and-rose-scented hair veiling my shoulders as we search the night sky. Mia sits in my lap, clinging to me like this is more than the moral support I keep trying to convince myself I'm giving.

My eyes scan the dusky horizon toward the compound for a moment. All it would take is one surprise visitor. One observant teammate scanning the perimeter, and I'm toast.

But Mia needs this, and I swore to myself I wouldn't let her down twice.

"You look worried, Maverick," she says softly, mint eyes dancing over my face.

"Not the most professional thing I've done in my life," I grumble, and she giggles.

"Sorry for making you step over the line. But—" Her voice quivers, and I don't regret any of this. "But I can't remember the last time I felt this safe."

I clear my throat, shifting uneasily. "Not even backstage ... the night we met?"

"Not even. After all, I was still reeling from getting tackled by you. You're no small man."

"No, ma'am."

"Ma'am. You make me sound old when you say that. Or like you're trying to put distance between us."

"That would be the smart thing to do," I counter.

"But for me? You'll make a sacrifice."

"Just this once."

"Thank you." Her hand comes up, stroking my bearded cheek, and I freeze, knowing in every inch of my body how dangerous this is.

"Your beard is softer than I thought it would be. Downright silky."

God, I love the feel of her fingers sliding through it, nails running lightly over my cheek. "Not every part of me's rough," I answer, not sure what else to say.

"You know everything about me now, Cowboy, but I know next to nothing about you."

"Cowboy?" I arch a brow.

"Figure if you can call me princess, it's only fair."

"You have a point," I concede on a one-way path to joblessness, "Princess."

I stare up at the sky, trying to focus on the constellations. The line of Orion's Belt that points to the Big Dipper, not the delicate fingers sending warm shivers up and down my spine.

"You still haven't answered me," she says after a long pause.

"Did you ask a question?"

"Not a question but a statement that deserves a response. Tell me about yourself."

"Not much to tell," I shrug, already turning inward,

though it's harder to do with this curvy woman wrapped in my arms.

"Tell me anyway."

I let out a low growl, like a warning. But Mia knows better. She smiles at my bluster, the kind of smile that invites me to say more.

"Most recently? Relocated from Texas. That's where I first started thinking about the whole bodyguard thing. Whole crew over there does the same kind of work. Before that, I was born and raised in southern Idaho near the Oregon border. Half farmer, half wild. Never quite belonged to either world."

"What do you mean?" she asks, like she already understands somehow.

"One side of my family: pioneer farmers—calm, steady, tied to the land. The other Shoshone-Bannock: wild as the ponies we ride—nomadic souls and bodies. Not tied to the land, embodying its blood and bones. Rodeo riders and aimless cowboys. Men who don't say much ... or need to."

Her grip on my neck tightens, like I'll drift away, vanish into the night. Maybe a part of me wants to because this— this intimacy?—is too much. Like I'm parting with a piece of my soul. The look in her eyes tells me she knows how to hold it, though.

Maybe that scares me even more.

"Men who don't settle down, I'm guessing?"

"That, too," I say, looking away. Not because I fear disappointing her, but because I fear, like getting me to talk, she could make me do even more. Maybe things against my nature.

She chuckles, her eyes sparkling with starlight. "I understand better than you think."

"How do you mean?" I ask gravely.

"I'm rootless, homeless, free as they come, and I hate it with a passion."

I nod.

She cocks her head. "Wait, you don't look like you believe me."

"Not that, Princess. I just know people always want what they can't have."

"Like alpacas and wool shops?"

"Maybe, though you could have them ... with a few sacrifices."

"Yes, I could, couldn't I?"

I don't know if she's asking me or the stars.

I swallow hard. "Something tells me you're capable of getting whatever you want. But first, you have to feel your own power."

She frowns, looking down at the porch, like she's really thinking through my words. Then, her eyes snap to mine. "When I'm with you, I feel powerful."

"That's not me, Mia."

"Then what is it?"

"You learning how to sit with silence."

She curls her hand into my shirt, and it takes every ounce of resolve not to bend my head, taste her pretty pink mouth. But she trusts me, and I refuse to violate that, no matter the cost.

"So, which are you, then? The steady farmer or the nomadic wild man?"

I scrutinize the stars, trying not to feel her warm breath on my cheek or the way her words make my heart ache for impossible things. "Until you? I was the man who followed orders without thinking." I say it like I don't want to admit it, but everything about it's the truth.

"So, I'm a bad influence, then?" She questions so softly I have to draw closer to make out the words.

"Not a bad influence. The catalyst I ignored to my detriment. Truth is, you can do everything right and still come out wrong."

I exhale slowly, unable to avoid her gaze any further, feeling more heat crawl up my neck than a Nevada night could ever deliver.

"Opposites again," she murmurs, eyes dropping to my mouth. "Because I'm the girl who's done everything wrong, hoping it's somehow going to turn out right."

Her words break something loose in my chest because I can tell, despite today's work, she still believes she's at fault for her life.

Before I can think, my hand comes up to stroke her feather-soft cheek. "You haven't done right or wrong, Mia, because you were never given the choice. But we're going to see what we can do about getting that back for you."

I don't move closer, don't let my eyes hunger for her mouth. Hell, I don't breathe.

This is the moment I lose plausible deniability. The moment there's no version of this I can explain away.

Moonlight and stardust dance across her face, and her head comes up slowly. Awkward lips touching mine for one breathless moment.

Her mouth is warm and unsure, like she's waiting to be told this is allowed.

Her first kiss, I'm pretty damn sure.

I don't back away, don't say half the things my mind is screaming ... about jobs and professionalism, propriety and what's right or wrong.

Instead, I let the magic exist—*linger*—as I return the

kiss with a quiet need that could destroy everything I've rebuilt.

CHAPTER
SIXTEEN

MIA

A fallout's coming, whether Maverick will name it.

I toss and turn beneath the soft quilts on the cabin bed, thoughts racing too fast to process. I scheduled my written statement to go out via social media six hours after Maverick read it.

The grandfather clock in the living room ticks ominously. The passage of each minute another step closer to freedom ... or ruin.

A square-cut jaw and soft beard. Warm mouth that confirmed my need. I touch my fingers to my lips, still remembering the kiss with Maverick.

It wasn't my first. But it was my only real one.

When I was sixteen, there was a backup dancer who I had a crush on. Jordan Miles. Eighteen years old and as adorable as they come. Behind the stage, we stole a moment together before security caught us and informed Edwin.

My manager raged, like I'd done something awful. Unforgivable.

Jordan thought he acted jealous. Like the old man wanted me for himself. But now I see it for what it was.

Isolation.

Edwin has always needed to keep me away from others. Away from connections.

Memories swirl in my head. *Your parents abandoned you. They're too selfish to care. They never ask about you.*

Accusations delivered by Edwin with the same calculated, surgical precision he used to fire Jordan. Nip it in the bud before I could form an attachment to another human being. Before I could find myself and my strength through another person.

I shift beneath the covers, heart pounding. A sweet torture to know Maverick sleeps on the other side of the wall. If he sleeps at all.

I close my eyes, imagine going to him. Imagine what it'd feel like to be in his powerful arms, firm heat steadying me.

When Edwin finds out, he'll stop this. Like he always does.

Unless I stop him first.

"And that's the reason for the statement," I whisper to myself.

At least, I followed my bodyguard's advice, didn't post the original video I intended to. The one I thought would tell my fans the truth, garner support. The one I'm pretty sure Edwin would have used to reframe everything around a lie.

That I'm unstable, mentally and emotionally. That I can't be trusted and my perceptions are off.

Floorboards creak in the living room, and my pulse pounds. He's awake, too. I rise quickly, wrapping myself in a purple silk robe and padding quietly into the living room.

Maverick stands in the kitchen, shirtless, the warm glow of the stovetop light washing over his chiseled flesh. Silvery raised flesh catches the light, a massive scar transecting an abstract black circle tattoo. My eyes trace the angry pucker of skin that breaks the shape, like the end of something.

He clears his throat, eyes steady, drawling, "Hope I didn't wake you."

"Couldn't sleep," I admit, taking a stool.

"Tea?"

I smile. He already knows my answer.

He moves around the kitchen quietly, muscles dancing beneath his tanned skin. A wild man with wander in his blood. The kind of guy who doesn't stay anywhere too long.

I grab my laptop, log into my social media account, and frown. It hasn't been six hours yet. It should post within the next half hour.

"Having second thoughts?" he asks, resting his hands on the counter.

"Yep," I squeak, trying to suppress the quiver in my voice.

He doesn't judge me. Doesn't say what to do. Just stands there like a strong boulder, like the only physical thing tethering me to what I want.

I drum my fingers on the countertop, meeting his steady gaze. "If I don't post it, none of this is real. You can go back to your life, your job. You can pretend this never happened."

He nods slowly, jaw clenched. "That what you want, Mia?"

I rub a hand over my face, sighing. "Maybe it's what makes the most sense. Maybe I've taken things too far. Made too big a deal out of Edwin and everything. Am I being ungrateful? Not thankful enough for all he's done for me?"

His brows furrow, and he exhales slowly. "The silence is worse than the noise would be."

The words, the way he looks at me, tell me he understands. "Tell me about the scar, your tattoo," I prompt.

He stares down at his chest for a long moment as if he's gathering his words around his gaze.

"Used to be on the rodeo circuit. A professional bull rider. PBR champ. Leaderboards. Dust, mud, fame. All of it."

"So, you were famous, too, then?"

He nods, staring at the countertop. "This," he says, tracing the thick silver line along his chest, "finished things for me. Shut the door on all my best-laid plans."

"And the limp?"

"Part of that, too. I'll spare you the gory details. But suffice to say, it was career-ending, life-shattering. Meant a medical discharge from the Guard, too." He stares away, sadness lingering in the black depths of his gaze.

I pull the laptop closer, staring at the screen determined. "Which is why I shouldn't do this. Not now. Not with you involved."

Surprise washes over his face for one flickering moment, like a candle catching flame.

I shake my head, seeing how selfish I've been all this time. "It's not lost on me that there will be hell to pay when this comes out. There will be questions about your involvement with me—with *this*."

"Mia, don't make a decision about your life and your future because of me—"

"Boone will want to know how much you knew about this," I whisper, "and you won't be able to lie because that's not who you are."

He reaches forward, presses the laptop shut, face solemn. "Decision's already made, right?"

I nod.

"Now we live with it." He pauses for one moment, studying the countertop. "Boone will hear about this later."

A high-pitched screech slices the air. The kettle. Angry, accusatory.

He extinguishes the burner, grabs mugs, fills mesh balls with loose-leaf tea. Blueberry and lavender fill the air as he fills the mugs.

The grandfather clock ticks and ticks and ticks.

He faces me, rounding the counter and sitting next to me. "You okay?" he asks, concern flooding his usually stoic face.

I twist my hands together, fingers voicing the anxiety I refuse to speak into existence. His big hand comes up, drops over mine, stilling them.

The clock still beats. The tea still steams. The lonely sound of a chuck-will's-widow carries somewhere off in the distance.

Or maybe it's something else.

His eyes fix on the window. His work never ends, but his gaze doesn't scan restlessly. Instead, he seems stuck on something. Some small detail I don't see.

"I'm afraid of how much this will cost you," I say in low tones, biting my bottom lip.

He straightens, face softening. "Already given me much more than it cost me, Mia Lowell. Maybe I'm not cut out for this bodyguard thing, anyway."

"Back to wandering, then?" I ask, voicing the ache behind my ribs. I know better than to indulge it, but it's still there.

He shrugs, turning his hand palm up and capturing my

fingers. "Don't want to think about the future right now. Just want to feel."

So, we sit in the silence until I'm certain it's too late.

Warm tears streak my cheeks, and I sniffle. He pushes the Kleenex box closer.

"This will force his hand," I say into the silence, like naming it might keep me steady.

———————

PEACH AND GOLD light threads through the curtains, the world still too quiet. But the air holds a rising heat that tells me everything's different now.

A faint buzz startles the big bodyguard, still holding my hand, and he eases to his feet. My palm is still warm where he comforted me as he eyes the screen of his phone, face going rock hard. "Excuse me while I take this outside."

I nod, throat tightening. On the other side of the door, I hear the rumble of his voice. I can't make out the words, but I can feel the force behind them. Not angry—unsettled.

I grab a tissue, dabbing at my eyes and cracking my laptop open again. The post is trending along with my name—both names. Comments crowd the screen. Most filled with alarm or concern. Some gaslighting. Others spewing lies and vitriol.

I am no longer invisible in this situation.

My phone is eerily silent. No texts. No calls. At least, not from Edwin or the other gray suits. It feels like the calm before a storm. Or maybe the eye of the hurricane.

Freedom. Sweet, easy. It won't last.

The front door swings wide, and Maverick steps back through, silently grabbing his button-down shirt from the couch and shrugging into it.

I devour his rugged frame before it vanishes beneath fabric, missing the intimacy of last night. Like it's already fractured. I wonder if I'll ever feel it with this man again. Or if I was chasing a dust devil all along.

"Did he call?" I ask breathlessly.

"You mean, Crowe?" the stern-faced cowboy asks, jaw muscle twitching. "Things have escalated."

"What do you mean?"

"Probably better to hear it straight from Boone. Still above my pay grade."

"Are you in trouble?"

He shrugs. "Don't worry about me."

"But, Maverick..."

The grandfather clock still ticks, and now I know, the clock on all of this has only just begun.

"Will you stay?" I ask, raising my chin.

"Yes, Mia," he answers.

"For how long?"

"Long as you want me," he answers, buttoning the top of his collar and then tucking in his shirt.

My cell phone lights up next to me: unknown caller. My hand hovers over it, tempted to answer, but I don't.

Last night, I mistook the silence for dread.

Today, I understand it was the last moment before everything learned how to scream.

CHAPTER
SEVENTEEN
MAVERICK

What if the bravest thing a man can do is not save a woman—but stand beside her while she burns down the cage?

I side-eye Mia as we drive in silence toward headquarters. Her face is a passive shield. But her hands work in her lap again, twisting, trembling, carrying everything bottled up inside.

She asked if I'd stay.

The one thing I can't guarantee. Only I said I would. And I mean to.

I don't know what the hell I'm thinking.

Her phone vibrates, and she pulls it out of her purse, holding it like it could sting her. The look on her face tells me it does.

"That Crowe?" I ask, already knowing.

"Unknown number." She sniffs.

"And what's he saying?"

"That medical professionals agree. It's time to end this. My making a scene, going to the public, only strengthens the conservatorship claim." She swallows loudly.

"It only has power if you believe it, Mia."

"Yeah," she sighs. I don't know if it's exhaustion or if she's second-guessing herself.

The red, ivory, and brown Nevada clay rolls by, fence-lined sage pastures with horses and cattle on either side. I long to reach out, grab her hand and calm her all over again. But not now.

Time to be a professional. To play things by the book, attempt to salvage what I can. Not push Mia into a situation she's not ready for. One she may be clinging to, just to feel safe.

At the compound, I round the vehicle, grinding my teeth against the chronic ache in my hip. Concentrating on not limping, though the joint's stiff and hurts like hell.

Boone meets us at the door, arms crossed. His face is cut from marble, not an emotion in sight. But I can feel the agitated energy pouring off him as he ushers us back to his office.

"Ms. Love," he says with a hand gesture toward a seat.

"Lowell," she corrects, straightening her posture. It means more than my boss can understand.

Leather squeaks as Boone sits behind his desk. The air smells of gun oil and old leather.

"I'll keep this brief and to the point," he says, resting his forearms on his desk. "Ms. Lowell, R&R's legal team, received a call this morning from Edwin Crowe informing us of an escalation."

A puff of air escapes her soft pink lips. Her eyes dart to me, searching. The corners of my mouth tip up. But my mind's going too fast for meaningful pleasantries.

"He's petitioning the court for an institutional review. Claiming your current behavior is linked to a complicated string of psychological diagnoses you've wrestled with for years."

She shakes her head, a low hiss escaping her. "Of course. Let me guess. Manic depression, borderline personality, suicidal ideation..."

Boone says, "I can't speak to the medical side of things. But Crowe's definitely making moves to get you back under his ... supervision."

Her voice shakes. "You mean, his control."

"Your parents are concerned. That's why they hired R&R Security. To get to the bottom of things."

"What do you mean?" she sniffs unimpressed.

"They came to us with concerns about your security," he explains. "Your relationship to your manager. A close call in Rhode Island before the incident here, and the fact Crowe may have taken out life insurance policies on you."

"Standard for performers," she counters, going pale.

"Maybe," Boone grumbles, unconvinced.

She stares at her fidgeting hands. "Don't let my parents convince you they care or that they're doing this for me." Ice threads her voice.

Boone counters, "They seemed very concerned about you when we spoke."

"Yeah, they're good at that," she spits out.

My boss grimaces. "After the shooting at the arena, they asked us to buy time, to try to get to the bottom of what's going on. But you haven't been very forthright."

Her head jerks up, and she eyes me, confused. Hurt stings her eyes, pales her cheeks. "Did you know about this?"

Her question throws me off. "Your parents hiring R&R Security? Of course."

"No. Did you know my parents wanted you to spy on me?"

I shake my head.

Her bottom lip quivers. "They're money grubbers. That's all they are. They don't care about me. Don't care about what I've done with my life—my achievements. They just want to rob me blind."

I straighten, placing my palms on my knees. "Those words don't sound like they came from you."

Her eyes flash with anger. But then, something deeper, sadder overtakes them. "Because that's what Edwin would say."

"Have you ever thought about why Crowe says those things?" I ask.

Boone's eyes dart between us. "I can step out?" he offers.

"No," Mia and I say at the same moment, then look away from each other awkwardly.

Silence.

Finally, Boone asks, "Do you have any other questions for me, Ms. Lowell?" Mia shifts uneasily but shakes her head. "In that case, we should probably wrap this up."

We stand.

But then, Boone adds, "Holt, I need to speak to you privately for a moment."

"Yes, sir."

"Mia, there's a conference room at the end of the main hallway with drinks and lunch. Please make yourself at home."

Her eyes flick to the door. Calculating. Bracing. Alone again.

Then, she glares at me for one breathless moment, like she can't make sense of any of this.

I step back, open the office door, and she passes through, body language stiff, silence brutal. I close it behind her and wheel back around, crossing my arms.

"Crowe's pulling out all the stops now."

"What else is there besides a psych eval?" I ask, head churning.

"He's floating a temporary injunction and a guardianship compliance review."

My hands fist at my sides.

"Her parents and their legal counsel might be able to buy her a few more days..."

I stare at the wooden desktop as if it holds the answers to the universe.

"But if she posts again—or speaks publicly—we may have to withdraw protection. If this becomes adversarial, R&R can't legally remain neutral."

"Understood."

He scrutinizes me, mouth twitching. "Anything else you need to tell me?"

Guilt washes over me like a tidal wave. Her journal entries. The communications she keeps getting. The statement I proofread and encouraged her to post. I should tell Boone everything.

"No, sir."

"Alright." His face is dark, conflicted.

I remain silent—not because the details are unimportant, but because they are not mine to give.

Mia hungers for agency. Freedom to make her own choices. How can I take that away from her without losing pieces of myself?

Still, I can tell by my superior's face that there will be hell to pay when Boone finds out.

A weight bears down on me as I leave his office. I just lied for Mia. No turning back now. But I didn't break her trust. I chose her.

EIGHTEEN

MIA

"**Y**ou've been quiet since we left headquarters.
What's going on?" Maverick asks back at the cabin.

"Nothing." My voice sounds far away, like I'm
floating above it. A flash of anger tightens my core. I bite
my lip.

He shifts uneasily.

"I need to use the restroom," I excuse.

When I return, overnight bag in hand, the kitchen stool
squeaks as Maverick jumps to his feet. I notice the subtle
way he favors one leg.

"What are you doing?" he growls.

"Leaving. I've caused enough trouble."

He grimaces, face reddening. His mouth works, but he
doesn't speak. He waits.

Rage rises in my chest.

"You're just like everybody else," I explode, dropping
my bag and pacing. "Another handler in boots."

His face storms, but he *still* says nothing, standing
strong, swallowing my fury.

"I should've known." I simmer. "My parents hired R&R —hired *you*—to pry into my life. To spy on me. God!"

The floorboards whine and squeak as my boots hammer across them. "And to think I confided in you. I *trusted* you. Maybe Edwin's right. Maybe I'm mentally incapacitated."

"Mia," he says low and dangerous.

I pause mid-stride, exhaling sharply.

Tension thickens the air until I can't breathe.

"Mia," he repeats, softer.

I shake my head, hands balled at my sides, cheeks heated.

Maverick doesn't move, doesn't defend himself or make excuses. Instead, he holds space for me, even when I rant and yell—accuse him of things I know aren't true.

But it's easier. Far easier than saying goodbye.

Tears stream down my face, and my shoulders droop as I try to hold it in. When he crosses the distance, when he wraps me in his steel-band arms, I break hard against his chest, trembling and sobbing.

Curling my fingers into his shirt, I plead, "Please, Maverick. Don't let them take me away. Don't let them take me from you."

I want him to say, *never*. To lie to me and make me feel better. Instead, he holds tighter, burying his face in my hair.

And that's when I know that I have to take a piece of him with me. No matter how much it hurts. Even if it wrecks me. I can't leave *without him*.

"Please, Maverick," I sob, clinging to him. "Pretend you love me. Show me how that feels, just once."

He pulls back, dark eyes wild. "I can't do that, Mia."

"Why not?" My voice trembles.

"Because it won't be pretend." The words are lightning.

Then, he's on me—hands gripping my face, mouth

seeking. Walking me backward. My shoulder blades hit the wall, head cradled by one hand. His tongue sweeps into my mouth, a growl rumbling through his chest. Passion ignites, wildfire behind my ribs.

He lifts me off the ground, and my legs wrap around his waist, hands gripping his neck.

"Need you," he grunts.

The backs of my eyes sting as he presses me hard against the wall, his firm length digging into my thigh. I gasp as he changes the angle, deepening the kiss.

A savage look fills his eyes, his hands roaming my body, claiming every inch. "We should stop," he grunts.

"No."

I rest my head against the wall, devouring him through tear-moistened lashes, etching him forever in my memory. The smell of pine. The heat of rock-hard muscles. The obsidian eyes that strip me down to my soul.

"But if I take this from you—"

"You can't take anything from me, Maverick, unless you say no."

That's when he decides, mouth crashing into me again, hands fighting with my clothes as we head down the hallway. He lowers me onto the mattress, face stern and beautiful, body straining to hold back.

Our gaze never breaks as I slide out of my jeans and shirt. Then, my bra and panties. He matches me item for item—denim and cotton, leather and steel—until nothing lingers between us but air.

His chest is broad and rippled, abs taut and defined. Threads of silver web near one hip, trauma branded in flesh. But it's his firm, veiny length, so taut it looks angry, that steals my breath.

"You're stunning, Mia," he says, raw-voiced, eyes sliding over me.

He pauses, swallowing hard. Then, he says, "I'm clean, and I have condoms."

My throat tightens, goosebumps lining my skin. *We're really doing this.* "No condoms," I pant. "I'm clean, too, and I need to *feel* you."

He moves with the agility of a puma. Muscles dancing beneath skin as he presses me into the bed, bracing with one arm—enough weight to reassure me I'm not alone.

His kiss is ignition. His calloused hands rake over my hips and waist. Then, up to my breasts. I gasp, his thumb sliding over one pebbled nipple. The breath hitches in his throat as he dips his head, burying me in the heat of his wicked mouth.

"Oh, God," I murmur, arching toward him. He swirls and devours, sucks and nips as his other hand descends lower, sliding between my legs.

"Mia." His voice is devotion. His fingers, a dangerous invitation, sliding and swirling. His thumb circles my clit, and I quiver. Need acute, I grind against him, begging.

His eyes meet mine—heat and fire. Fingers claim me as I gasp, squirm.

"Easy," Maverick says against my mouth, hot breath brushing my cheek. "Trust me, Princess."

My eyes slide shut. Heat curls and twists, melting into his touch. Warm lips feather down my ribcage, trailing fire. Excruciating. Slow.

He slides lower. I tremble, a live wire at his touch.

Shouldering between my legs, his head dips. I dissolve into bliss. Breath racing. Body unraveling.

And, God, how he moves—slow, savoring, claiming.

His thick tongue is wet velvet, pushing me to the edge.

My hips buck, desperate. He's on me, inside me ... circling, stroking, until I throb, dizzy and aching.

Desire hums through me. Pleasure sharp as a knife's point.

Then, I shatter.

The world falls away. My voice echoes through the cabin. No control. Just the cowboy with dark eyes and steady hands.

He palms my cheek—*seeing*—truly seeing me. "You okay?"

"More than okay," I whisper. "Better than—" I can't speak.

"Oh, yeah?" He chuckles huskily. "Need a break?"

"No, Maverick," I whisper, clutching his neck. "I need more—*you*."

"I don't want to hurt you."

"Then, don't stop." I stretch up, capturing his mouth.

He rolls onto his back, pulling me with him. His thick cock digs into my leg as I straddle him.

"Want you to ride me, Mia. Take what you need from me. I won't hold anything back."

Our eyes lock. I rise, grip his girth, and slowly inch over him.

Too much. I grimace.

His hands grip my hips, guiding me back. "Slow and easy, Princess. Don't rush this."

I stroke his cheek, love radiating from my eyes. This time, I savor him, sliding up and down. Exploring. Accepting. Trusting.

His hands draw me lower as desire builds. Steadying me when I squeeze my eyes tight.

Exhale.

Drawing us closer... until we breathe, move as one.

I whimper, body shaking. Pain and passion unite. I lean forward, hearts pressing together, lips tangling as I fly free, spasming and breaking.

He drives deep with a throaty cry, burying waves of warmth.

Afterward, I trace the circle tattoo on his chest, wrapped in tenderness. I've never felt so cherished—so seen. I almost don't know how to hold it. Still, I can't let go.

The bedroom is dark, like a lantern's been extinguished. The world outside has slipped fully into night.

Maverick cradles me in his arms like nothing could tear me away.

And yet, it's still there between us—the inevitable.

I rest my head on his chest, the loud thud of his heart against my ear. It could almost convince me there's a way through this.

His hand comes up, cupping my cheek, his fingertips brushing the wet track of my tears. He tilts my face toward his, and that's when I see his eyes are red, too. He wants me to see it.

He swallows hard. "This circle's us now," he says, like a promise—though uncertainty threads his voice.

I can't speak. I only nod, nestling against him.

CHAPTER
NINETEEN

MAVERICK

The world is still—shrouded in the night's calm. The moment before things wake. Before the noise begins.

Mia's buttery curls radiate from the pillow like the sun's first rays on a winter morning. Her breath slow and steady, cheeks pink with sleep.

I shift carefully, trying not to wake her. I reach for my cellphone on the side table, knowing I'll find messages I don't want to read.

I clench my jaw, scrolling through Boone's texts.

> Bring Mia back in. Everything's changed.

"What is it?" the beauty next to me asks, groggy-voiced. Her face is peace and safety. Can't take them from her yet.

"I'll make coffee, breakfast."

Her hand palms my chest, fingers tracing the circle that's ours now.

"No matter what happens, right?" Her bottom lip trembles.

110

I press my hand over hers, feeling the weight on my heart. "No matter what."

She inhales, steeling her expression. "Coffee, then, and breakfast. Sounds good."

I grasp her hand, bring her fingertips to my mouth, and kiss them slowly. One at a time until the heat rises in her cheeks.

"You're the only good I've found in this world, Mia. In a long, long time."

She licks her lips, face etched in resolve. Rose and plum linger—a knowing that settles deep. Something I have to hold on to come what may.

I sit on the edge of the bed, regaining my senses and my head.

Last night.

Fuck.

Never should've happened. Never will regret it. Hope she won't either.

Her arms thread around my waist, warm breath nestled at my neck. Wish I had answers. She kisses my cheek, then let's go.

I dress in silence as she watches, blanket pressed to her chest, putting distance between us.

"You're already leaving, aren't you," she murmurs. Not a question.

I lean toward her, stroking her décolletage and letting the silk of her hair slide between my fingers.

"If this goes where it's headed... I won't be allowed to stay." The words come out dull but weighted. Thudding hollow in the space between us.

"I know," she sniffles.

There's no anger or recrimination, just resignation. That scares me more.

On the wings of the pre-dawn morning, an owl hoots. My body tenses, and her questioning gaze meets mine.

But she doesn't name the interruption. Neither do I. A silent witness to quiet pain. A part of the circle, too, though I don't want it to be.

As I head for the kitchen to work on food, my body strains. Every cell wants to rush in to protect her. Do something dramatic, decisive. But I can't take away her agency. Or fight her fights ... unless she asks.

Not acting wrecks me. A torture I can barely hold, though I do it for her.

Floral, smoky notes fill the air when she shuffles into the kitchen and takes a seat. I push a mug of coffee in her direction, already storming with cream.

She watches it raptly, swallowing hard. Then, she opens her laptop and starts scrolling. I read the fallout on her face, illuminated by the screen's glow—pain, relief. Maybe fear, though she hides that better.

"Fan comments. Influencer reactions and stitches. News outlets, comedians." She bows her head.

"Want to talk about it?" I ask.

She shakes her head, sniffling.

Silence fills the room. But the grandfather clock still ticks. The crickets still chirp. Life never stops.

"What is this?" she asks suddenly, wrinkling her nose when I hand a plate piled high with eggs, bacon, and golden-fried potatoes to her.

I shrug. "Cowboy breakfast."

"I'll blow up like a cow if I eat like this." She shakes her head, pushing her fork around on the plate. "So many carbs. So many calories."

Her voice is strong but distant, like she's falling back

112

into old patterns. My chest squeezes at the thought, so tight I almost can't breathe.

"Do you want to eat like this?" I ask. A simple question.

She freezes as if she doesn't understand. Suddenly, mischief dances in her eyes. "Do you have ketchup?"

I rifle through the fridge, then place the red bottle in front of her.

She claps her hands together. "Then, hell, yeah, I want to eat like this, just once."

Just once. Like last night.

I round the counter, sitting next to her, so our knees touch. "What you want doesn't have to be *just once*, you know?"

Her cheeks go pink. "Are you flirting with me, Mav?" Bittersweet threads through her voice.

"Reminding you," I answer, leveling my gaze on hers.

She nods, feeling the sudden heaviness of the moment.

"I won't forget."

I'm counting on that. But I don't say it. The last thing Mia needs is more pressure.

BOONE SITS BEHIND HIS DESK, jaw tense. "The conservatorship hasn't been dissolved ... yet. But an emergency advocacy group has stepped in. They're citing a conflict of interest. Maybe enough to freeze Crowe's authority, at least, temporarily."

Mia shifts in her seat, side-eyeing me before looking down. Hope flickers, though she says in low tones, "He won't give up that easily."

"No, but a judge has stepped in, allowing legal counsel for you and housing pending review."

I straighten, bracing for impact.

Boone's forehead furrows as he scrutinizes me. "Not here. At a property associated with the advocacy group."

"Oh," she huffs, fingers twisting in her lap. My hands ache to comfort her.

"Holt, take her back to the cabin, help her pack her things. Jack'll be around in about an hour to collect her."

Mia's eyes snap to me, her mouth working.

Boone's eyes narrow. "There a problem?"

"No," I say flatly. "But her safety. Has the court weighed in on that?"

"No longer an R&R matter," he grits out between clenched teeth. "Will need to regroup with you later about ... next steps."

"Next steps?" I ask.

He grimaces, running a hand through his hair. "A new assignment. Away from *this*."

Boone delivers the last words like he knows. Guilt tangles behind my chest, a fast-growing vine thick with thorns.

"So, the judge didn't rule in Edwin's favor?" the curvy blonde says next to me, like she's still trying to process everything.

"No."

"And I can have an attorney?" She arches a perfectly trimmed eyebrow. Her hands twist. "Edwin still controls my finances, though."

Boone clears his throat, glaring at me. "The court will have to sort that out. All I know is the advocacy group has offered representation—pro bono. They'll be able to tell you more."

She presses her palms against her knees, stilling them.

"Okay," she says softly. "Then, there's a light at the end of the tunnel. Maybe."

He nods slowly. "Your parents would like to see you at some point, Mia. Be prepared."

WE DRIVE IN SILENCE, my heart breaking at the thought of her doing all of this alone. But she doesn't need a savior. She needs steady, strong, patient. I can be those for her.

Mia doesn't take long to pack, her overnight bag still full from last night. The clock gives us forty more minutes. Not nearly enough.

I tangle my fingers with hers, leading her back to the bedroom and privacy. The quiet fills the empty spots between us as I hold her, sinking my head into her hair, breathing her in. Trying to remember this for always.

"I need you to be strong, Princess."

She nods, fingers curling in my shirt and drawing me closer.

Our lips meet, heat and longing pressed between us. "Not Princess," I say firmly, fingers sliding into her hair, dividing her locks without thinking. "Warrioress. Fighter."

"Ass kicker," she says in watery tones.

"Don't I know it," I grumble, plaiting her silky strands between fingers that remember.

When Jack comes earlier than he's supposed to—as I expected he would—I carry her bag to the vehicle. Our eyes say everything our mouths can't, pulses synced in the space before forgetting.

Only I know I won't. Ever.

She wears my golden braids as the truck pulls out, sunlight catching in the strands.

I brace against the porch railing, exhaling slowly, as the truck disappears in a red dust cloud.

The consequences of every choice I've made since my first bodyguard job settle heavy in my chest.

The screen door squeaks. Floorboards whine as I step back into the cabin, prepared to wash away every trace of Mia—*and the man she changed.*

CHAPTER
TWENTY

MIA

"**M**s. Lowell," the woman with gentle eyes greets. "I'm Mrs. Everley." She steps forward, offering her hand.

I nod without returning the gesture, shrinking inwardly —unready to face the world or my celebrity again.

But the fifty-something woman with a gray-streaked mahogany bob doesn't rush me. She doesn't say a thing as I sit across from her in the office, and she folds her hands together.

"Welcome." Her voice is smoky and soft as a whisper, but there's a quiet steel running through it. My shoulders relax.

"Thank you."

"We'll start with a review of your medications, any prescriptions we may need to fill," she says, typing on her laptop.

"Is this confidential?" I ask, brows knitting.

"Absolutely. And optional, too. We want to make you feel safe and comfortable here. Whatever that may look like for you."

I open my mouth, but nothing comes out. Instead of twisting my arms in my lap, I bring one up, fingering the braid. I can almost feel Maverick with me. A quiet kind of strength.

"I haven't been on anything for the past..." I pause, eyeing her. Weighing whether I can trust her. "The past few months, and I feel fine. Even mood. Clear head."

"Does your doctor know about these changes?"

"Not the doctor or therapist Edwin makes me go to. No."

"And you say you're feeling better?"

"Yes, like I can finally think for myself."

She smiles, not cloying or fake. But like my words have hit some chord she recognizes.

"And how are your moods? Any sadness? Thoughts of self-harm."

I shake my head, choosing my words carefully. "Before the incident, when R&R Security stepped in, I sometimes felt helpless. Like a hamster on a wheel. Like I have no say in my own life."

She nods, eyes warm but cautious. "Our legal team is still reviewing the conservatorship. But from what I've seen, your feelings are justifiable."

"All I wanted was a break. A stop from the touring, the performing, a moment to breathe. Especially after the shooting. If anyone had been injured on account of me..."

"Or if you'd been hurt," she urges.

I pause, letting the words sink in. Sadness floods me, stinging the backs of my eyes. "You're right," I say suddenly, eyes searching hers. "You speak to me like I'm a human being—not a commodity."

"Because you are," she answers, expression determined. "And you have been all along."

I nod, swallowing hard.

Fingers glide through my hair all over again. A gruff voice rumbles next to me, reassuring me—not saying goodbye.

"Dinner's served at six. Here's a copy of the menu." She leans across the table, handing a laminated paper to me.

"If you need anything, don't hesitate to call. A housekeeper comes through once a day to check on things, and we'll also be checking in with you regularly to meet court requests and to facilitate your case."

"I can't thank you enough," I whisper.

"The grounds are secure and heavily monitored, and your room has a small private patio, if you'd prefer to avoid other residents. But everyone here is very welcoming, not intrusive."

"Other residents?" Panic grips me.

She nods, the corners of her mouth turning up. "Other high-profile women in need of assistance. Whether it's the wife of a politician going through an abusive divorce or an actor transitioning from rehab. You'll find many like-minded women here. People who understand, but only when you're ready."

"Okay." I exhale.

"In that case, let me show you to your room. I'll assume you can shower and go about daily activities without supervision?"

Her question startles me. "Yes."

A single sheet of paper slides across the desk with a pen.

I eye it suspiciously. *Is she really asking me to sign paperwork?* I'm used to autographs, not decisions ... or consent.

"There will be more where that came from, but I'll walk you through everything later. This acknowledges that you understand the house rules and have accurately self-reported your current physical and mental states. And it also provides a waiver for medical intervention if needed."

My hand hovers over the paper, pen suspended in mid-air.

"What do you mean, medical intervention?"

"If there's ever an emergency. Some reason an ambulance might need to be called."

My eyes scan the paper, seeing places to initial and then sign related to first responders, resuscitation, a life directive.

"If you'd prefer to hold off on signing that until you can consult our legal team, that's fine, too. The intricacies of your case are such that it might make more sense."

I smile bitterly. "You mean that I'm uncertain whether I can make these decisions at all?"

She nods. "Hopefully, that will change sooner than later."

"Hopefully," I repeat, scanning the sheet of paper. "What's the date?" I ask as I initial and sign it.

"The sixteenth."

The signature comes out too scrawled and flashy. I'm used to signing in metallic Sharpie, not a ballpoint pen. But it feels good. The brush of my hand across the paper. The sense, though fleeting, that I belong to me and me alone.

She stands rounding the desk and sweeping her hand to follow. "Let me show you to your room."

A staff member follows behind, carrying my overnight bag. He disappears as she shows me around the secluded room with a private bathroom and modest-sized television.

Instead of feeling like they're closing in on me, the walls are a kind of freedom that ripens with each breath, each step I take. But beneath these minor victories is a bittersweet ache only Maverick can fill.

My raven-haired cowboy bodyguard. I wonder what he's doing now as I run my fingertips across the dining room table, mind wandering back to heat and breath.

"Your parents have requested a meeting," Mrs. Everley says.

I brace my hands on the table, anger simmering beneath the surface. But it feels softer somehow, less powerful and dangerous in the light of day.

"When?"

"Whenever you're ready. They would like to discuss your living arrangements and legal needs."

I want to cross my arms and stubbornly refuse their help. After all, they abandoned me. But if it weren't for them, I would never have worked with R&R or met Maverick.

"Maybe this afternoon? Before dinner?"

"Yes, after I've had a little time to settle in."

THREE HOURS LATER, I enter a minimally furnished conference room, eyeing my parents with a frown.

My mother's face blanches. Dad shifts awkwardly, like he can't decide whether he should sit or stand.

Mrs. Everley waves me to a seat, then takes the one next to me. "Ms. Lowell, I want to start by explaining that your parents requested this meeting. I'll be mediating, and you should feel free to leave at any time."

Anger and skepticism wrestle behind my ribs as I eye my parents. Both older than I remember. But a flicker of curiosity makes me ask, "How did you get here so quickly?"

Dad lives in Nashville and Mom in Las Vegas.

"Is it okay if we talk?" Dad addresses Mrs. Everley, shifting in his seat.

She nods.

His eyes meet mine. "You've been all over the news, Mia. The incident in Rhode Island, the shooting here. Your disappearance. Then, Crowe started calling..."

Mom adds, "I've been worried sick about you. I didn't expect much. But a call—*from you*—would have been nice."

"So would a childhood," I answer, narrowing my eyes.

"See, Teddy?" Mom glares at Dad. "Always blaming me for everything."

"I didn't come here for a fight," he hisses, frowning.

"But you saw it yourself—"

Mrs. Everley intervenes, tiny voice surprisingly loud. "I would like us to stay on topic, please. *And to take our turns.*"

"I'm not here to defend myself," Dad continues. "But after the statement, I had to intervene. See what your mom and I can do to help."

Mom's mouth twitches. "Yes, Mia. We want to help," she seconds, voice breaking slightly. "But only if you want it."

"Everything I need, I already have," I whisper, staring at the table. But when my eyes dart from one face to the other, it hits me all at once. This is not the time or place for stubborn independence. I need allies, no matter where they come from.

"Are you sure?" Mom says.

I shake my head, fingering the hem of my dress. "I don't want to make any decisions today. But I would like to talk again. Not about the past. Not about the things that can't be changed. I want to explore how we can work together to overturn the conservatorship."

Dad's eyes narrow; Mom's mouth thins to a line.

Ultimately, none of this would have happened if they hadn't signed away their parental rights. But we're past the point of blame and controversy. Now, I need an army to fight Edwin Crowe, even if that requires swallowing my pride.

After the meeting, I unpack half of my overnight bag, filling the empty dresser in the bedroom. The carpet is rose-pink shag, luxurious beneath my bare feet.

I find the flannel from the cabin neatly folded. My hands slide over it, remembering. When I shrug into the impossibly soft fabric, I instantly relax. It smells of pine and strength—Maverick.

Then, I go back to the bag, locating yarn and a crochet hook. My eyes snag on something else, too—lavender blueberry tea. Maverick must've added it to the bag along with his shirt.

I sigh, eyeing my phone, wishing things could be different. But I can't risk causing him more trouble. The awkward meeting with Boone this morning said it all. He knew more than he let on.

Instead, I head for the kitchen to boil water. Then, I sit at the table, singing and crocheting.

For the first time, the silence doesn't feel like punishment. It feels like room to breathe.

CHAPTER
TWENTY-ONE
MIA

S oft golden threads of light bleed through the curtains. I snuggle deeper into the covers, finding warmth and the ache of loneliness.

My fingers go to my lips, still remembering—*dark eyes, muscular arms, a steady, quiet presence.*

I reach for a braid, fingers grazing over the orderly plaits. Not a dream.

I wonder what my bodyguard's doing today. Up before dawn. Coffee and cowboy breakfast. My stomach rumbles at the thought.

In the bathroom mirror, I expect to see a fragmented girl. One who still believes Crowe's lies.

Instead, I find a woman who survived the night. No shame. No regret.

I unbraid my hair slowly in the shower, running my hands through the yellow waves. I can almost feel Maverick's fingers in my hair, his hot breath on my cheek.

Afterward, I dress in comfortable clothes that feel like a hug. My favorite pair of jeans. A soft pink sweatshirt. Hair in a ponytail, face free of makeup. I hesitate by the door.

I could remain secluded. Take breakfast alone in my room. But it's not what I want. As long as I can decide for myself, I'm going to.

I half expect stares or whispers when I enter the common space lined with tables and filled with savory and sweet smells. Instead, the other women remain present but distant. Soft smiles and nods of the head. A group invites me to sit with them.

No side-eyeing, no gossip. Normalcy without pressure.

The clink of forks against plates. A gentle hush of laughter. Pastries proudly made by Sweet Sage Bakery, a local establishment.

Quiet. Normal. I soak it in.

This is what safety looks like when no one's watching for cracks.

As breakfast concludes and servers come around to collect plates, I spy Mrs. Everley heading in my direction. Her stride is crisp, all business. I stand, and she meets me halfway.

"Good morning, Ms. Lowell. Was breakfast to your liking?"

Not a cowboy breakfast.

"Fine, thank you." I smile thinly.

"You're just the woman I was looking for," she continues brusquely. "Shall we head back to my office?"

Inside, behind closed doors, she leans on her desk, facing me, arms crossed. "I wanted to provide you with a quick procedural update."

"Oh," I sigh, stomach tightening.

"Our legal team has officially signed on as emergency counsel, and Edwin Crowe has been barred from direct contact with you. Your financial access remains restricted but under review. More importantly, so does Mr. Crowe's."

I almost can't believe my ears. Fear and apprehension pulse through me. I press my lips tightly together.

"What's that look for?" Mrs. Everley asks, rounding her desk to take a seat.

I swallow hard. "Just can't believe this is really happening. That I may stand a chance of gaining control of my life again."

She smiles warmly.

I add, "I know it's no fantasy or promise of instant freedom. But it feels tangible, like I could have a say in my future."

She nods firmly. "This is a lot to go through, psychologically and emotionally. Do you have an outlet for your thoughts and feelings? Maybe journaling?"

"Yes, I've always kept a detailed journal, documenting everything."

A lightbulb goes on in Mrs. Everley's head. "Does our legal team know about your journal? Could it be used to corroborate your allegations against Crowe?"

I don't have to think. "Yes, I wrote everything down, sometimes in great detail. And I have other proof, too."

The corners of her mouth tip up. "Let's get an appointment scheduled with the legal team. I'm certain they would like to know more."

Once, such a request would have terrified me. Certain Edwin's punishment would far outweigh any good I could gain from reporting on him. But everything feels different now...

I twirl a stray curl around my finger, already missing the braids.

...*because of Maverick.*

"I would also like you to speak with our forensics contact when you have a moment. Our legal team needs

126

clarification about some finance-related patterns that they've noticed and also activity regarding life insurance policies."

My stomach knots. "I know nothing about my finances or insurance. Those decisions were made without me."

"I see," she says, knitting her forehead. "All the more reason to call him." She pushes a business card across the table toward me; I pocket it.

Outside, a slight breeze makes early afternoon bearable. I walk to my building slowly, staring up at the immense periwinkle sky punctuated by a handful of fluffy white clouds. My mind races. Forensics. Finances. Legal advocacy.

Up ahead, I hear a lonely sound. Like a hooting owl, only softer, more gentle. A lone mourning dove perched on the fence. It doesn't fly off when I sit nearby, leaning back against the fence on the cool manicured grass.

It sees me without being afraid. The silent witness to my choosing.

I dig the card out of my pocket and make the call. A gruff voice answers after I'm patched through by the receptionist.

"This is Mia Lowell, and I'm calling with one question. Can you help me understand where my money went?"

By the end of the call, I have no assurances, and my hands shake. But I do have a mounting case against Edwin. The kind that might finally bring his house of cards to the ground.

In my room, I sit at the table listening to music and crocheting. I eye my cell phone atop the kitchen counter, longing burgeoning.

The braids are gone. I could almost convince myself R&R and Maverick were a dream. Except soft wool threads around my fingers. I rise to make another cup of tea, the cozy comfort of blueberries and lavender snaking through the air.

I check my cell phone as I walk past, heart jumping into my throat for one moment. Until I see Maverick hasn't called.

But Boone has texted.

> You able to come out for a debriefing off the books tomorrow? I can send a driver around?

My chest squeezes tight; I can't breathe. My fingers hover over the phone, desperate to ask about Maverick.

But no, I can't.

Then, another text comes through.

> Josie would love to see you again, too.

I can't say no to that.

Night falls, and I snuggle under the flannel beneath a fluffy blanket, putting the finishing touches on a crochet fox.

Music plays softly in the background.

Not mine. No performances. No pressure.

I almost don't know what to do with myself.

But I do know one thing. The thing I whisper to myself in the cozy quiet of my new space.

"I'm still here."

CHAPTER

TWENTY-TWO

MIA

Morning starts with a breve latte to-go from the on-site restaurant, greeting other residents as I pass. I sip the creamy drink, walking toward Mrs. Everley's office. Despite the early hour, the summer day already promises to boil.

I wear a pair of light-washed Ariats and a white tank top with beige embroidered cowboy boots. A long silver circle and turquoise necklace hangs low, echoing the scar-bound tattoo—*and its owner*—that I can't get off my mind.

One week in cowboy country, and I'm already going Western. It's the least remarkable of the changes I've experienced here, though.

I check in with the administrative assistant and wait. He raps softly on the door, and I hear Mrs. Everley's voice. "Come in."

The blinds are drawn, tranquil music playing. Incense burns on her desk, a smoky sweetness edged with patchouli, and a small water feature in the corner babbles like a brook.

I didn't notice these things the day I arrived. Can't

figure out how I missed them, now. But my mind raced, my heart broken. And I couldn't see past my own problems.

"Ms. Lowell, you look like you fit in now," she says, standing to shake hands.

I settle in the chair across from her with a shrug. "I could maybe get used to this place. Beautiful skies, a lonesome prairie, rugged mountains."

"Cute cowboys," she says with a giggle that catches me completely by surprise.

"Well, if you say so." Though I play it cool, one man haunts my mind.

"Don't suppose you're here to talk about that," she says, mouth firming. "More like an update?"

My throat tightens, chest heavy.

"Do you want the good or bad news first?"

"Good." My voice comes out firmer than before.

"I touched base with the legal team earlier, and Crowe's authority remains paused, though not revoked."

I nod, feeling cold silver and turquoise between my fingers as she talks.

"But based on the evidence you've provided." She shakes her head. "It's only a matter of time before the judge rules in your favor."

"Really? You think so?" I ask, pulse pounding.

"I can't predict the future. But your case looks solid. Airtight."

I relax my shoulders. "And the hearing is still set for the thirtieth?"

"Yes," she says, typing. Then, she looks up. "The forensic audit is officially underway, and the legal team continues to review your journal for additional documentation."

"Are they finding what they need?"

"And then some. You didn't spare a detail." The corners of her mouth soften, tilting up. "Crowe has retained his own counsel, and he's pushing hard behind the scenes."

I nod, licking my lips. "As expected."

"This isn't over. It's just moved underground. If we need to move it back out into the light again, I trust you'll be ready."

"Always," I say, and for the first time since the concert in Rough & Ready Country, there's force behind my words.

"Another meeting with your parents is scheduled for later this week, and you said you were going to meet with Boone at R&R Security?"

"Today, actually," I say, looking down at my phone.

My heart skips for a second until I see there are no missed calls or new texts. Been this way all week. But I know Maverick's the kind of man who does things right. That means at the right time, too.

"Soon. Shoot, I didn't realize what time it is," I excuse.

"In that case, don't let me keep you."

I stand, and she comes around her desk to shake hands. "You've taken major steps since arriving here, Mia. Not only fighting back but also providing evidence and information. You've also proven you're healthy, stable, and capable of making your own decisions."

"Thank you." I grin. And I've proven I know how to be silent when that's what life asks for.

An hour later, Jack pulls up in his truck, and my heart sinks. Though I know better, part of me still hoped for a big black pickup and a quiet, dark-eyed driver.

"Hope you don't mind country," he says as he drives. Learned a week ago that's as far as conversation goes with him.

Didn't respond back then, braids in my hands, heart

limping along. But today, I have an opinion. "It's growing on me."

"Comes with the boots," he grumbles. "All you need now is a Stetson."

"Give it another week," I murmur, sarcasm threading my words.

When I see the massive ranch gate—iron, wood, and stone—a hummingbird lands in my chest. I swallow hard, trying not to hope. But hope isn't something you can capture or ignore.

Staring out at the distant prairie, I imagine Maverick walking the perimeter, slight limp, eyes narrow and scanning. Body taut and ready for trouble.

Boone and Josie greet me at the Ranch door.

"Mia!" the bubbly teen screams.

"Josie," I lean down, hugging her close. "So good to see you again, though I swear you've grown since the last time I saw you," I observe, eyeing the too-short hem at the bottom of her jeans.

"Like a weed," Boone chuckles.

We head inside for the debriefing while Josie hangs back, catching crickets in the tall grass. Nothing is monumental. Just going over timelines, filling in details, aligning narratives, and providing contact information.

Afterwards, we stand outside. Josie scrambles into a sprawling ancient oak. Its thick, gnarled branches nearly touch the ground.

Still, I watch the teen, holding my breath.

"You okay?" he grunts.

"Not a fan of heights," I confess, holding a hand to my chest. "For myself or anyone else."

"How'd you manage all that flying you must've done as a touring act, then?"

The question feels remote, like it's not meant for me. But for another time and place.

I smile sheepishly, confessing, "Sedation. There was a pill for everything back then."

"Not so long ago," he corrects, kicking the red dirt in front of him.

"I don't want to go back."

"I know," he says with a nod. "Sounds like between the advocacy group and your parents, what you want is getting more likely with each passing day."

"Most of it anyway," I say in low tones, pushing sadness deep. "And things here at R&R, are they okay?"

He shrugs.

"I know there were concerns about the possible legal repercussions of helping me."

He removes his Stetson, stabbing his fingers into his hair. "Par for the course. It's why we have a legal team, Ms. Lowell."

"And Maverick Holt? Is he okay?" I ask before I can stop myself.

Boone stills, eyes narrowing like he's reading me. "Fine."

It's already too late. I've said too much, so I keep going. "Is he here by chance?"

He replaces his cowboy hat, face unreadable.

Josie squeals, jumping down from the branch where she stands, nearly making me scream. My knees shake just watching her antics.

"You look pale all of a sudden, Ms. Lowell," he observes with a chuckle.

Josie runs over, tugging on his sleeve. "Dad, are you going to tell her about the ranch or not?"

Our eyes meet, and he frowns. "The newbie's out ranch

shopping in Red Mesa. Good land there, no neighbors for miles. Abundant water rights. Peace. Quiet."

My pulse pounds, though I try to play it cool.

Boone frowns, adding, "If you happen to be in the area … that would be your choice."

If Jack is okay with a detour. Not sure I'll give him the choice.

I smile. "Then, I'd like to go."

Back in his truck, country music's the topic of conversation.

"You gonna start singing cowboy songs?" Jack asks.

I freeze, unsure of my answer. "Never got to choose what I sing," I realize out loud. "Maybe it's time to start."

He nods, whistling along to the radio as the landscape shifts from golden fields to rusty rock formations. Every shape and size, like nature's an abstract sculptor.

"Red Mesa," he says. "Good ranch country."

I nod, throat too thick to speak as I stare at the horizon, distance narrowing. Until I can almost feel my cowboy bodyguard.

We stop in front of the only ranch with a "For Sale" sign —a big, black truck parked next to it.

"Need me to wait?" he asks.

"No, I've got my phone handy and can call for a ride," I answer breathlessly.

"Best of luck to you, ma'am."

"Thank you, Jack."

My hands are still for the first time I can remember. Waiting for something that's not a promise... but possible.

CHAPTER
TWENTY-THREE

MIA

Heat shimmers across brown clay and minty sage. Katydids roar like mini rattlers. The wind sweeps through the tall grass on the edge of the property.

Anticipation burgeons behind my ribs.

I don't know whether he's here. Yet, I feel him to the marrow of my bones.

In the distance, verdant green parses the golden plains. Row upon row of lines, emerald vines snaking upward around wire and twine. Pea or bean plants if I had to guess.

Shading my eyes against the sun, I stare up through the rows. They have to be a good twenty feet tall, maybe more. They cast columns of shade in the surrounding grass, swishing and swaying with the breeze, bathing me in momentary cool as I walk the line.

Silvery irrigation ditches run next to them, cooling the surrounding land.

A fat robin darts between vines, warbling and warning as I draw closer. Must have a nest nearby. A painted bunting flits past, riotous feathers giving it away. A luminous hummingbird hovers low, beak dipping toward my hair.

I laugh under my breath, swatting the iridescent beauty away. "My hair's not a flower," I scold.

Then, I see him.

Off in the distance, a tall man paces. Slight limp, beige hat slung low over dark eyes. He walks between fence posts, measuring them with his stride. Then, testing wire, hands working. More a rancher than a bodyguard, his measured movements and silent gaze attest.

I walk between the emerald trellises, breath held, catching glimmers of the big man between each row. He appears, disappears. Again and again, as my throat tightens, and I mentally string words together.

Don't know if I'll be able to speak. Breath already stuttering, pulse racing.

I touch the silver circle necklace, cool turquoise, to steady myself.

Suddenly, he stops, stills for a long, silent moment. As if he senses a change in the wind.

I wait, holding my breath. Uncertain if I've made the right move coming here.

He turns slowly, scanning the green strands until our eyes meet. They lock.

He doesn't smile. Doesn't speak. Just stares for a breathless moment that stretches forever.

I open my mouth. My voice fails me.

Then, he bows his head, takes a step toward me. Hesitates, resting his hands on his hips. "Didn't know if you'd come."

"I didn't know if I was allowed."

A flash of teeth, a steady smile—he crosses the distance to me. I hold my breath, walking on one side of the vines, him on the other, catching flickers of each other between vegetation until we meet at the end in pastoral fields stretching off toward the horizon in all directions.

"Good soil. Alfalfa proves it," he says.

I nod, side-eyeing the cowboy—breathing in pine soap and that something darker I can't get enough of. He's taller than I remember, though it's only been days. His face square-cut and rugged, his body a wall of muscle.

"Good water access. Fencing mostly decent." He removes his hat, swiping the back of his hand over his forehead. "Strong windbreaks and the shelter of mountains mean it's quiet most of the time. A natural shelter from twisters."

"And these," I say, finally finding my voice, striding toward the long lines of green. "Peas, beans, whatever. They grow beautifully."

"Hops," he says, warm eyes dancing over my face. "Nothing happens the first year. Growth takes time. Don't see payoff immediately, but they come back stronger each season."

We continue silently along the uneven ground. Only inches apart but not touching.

I push my hair off my face, fighting the welcome breeze. Just enough to cool the perspiration kissing my arms.

Maverick stops, eyes veering off to one side. Then, he gestures, drawls slowly, "Thinking alpaca stables over there where we can take advantage of the afternoon shade from the cottonwoods. And maybe," he points to a spot not far from the ranch house, "a wool shop over there."

The world slows.

Maverick nods once, eyes simmering. Smile boyish and unguarded.

My hand goes to my chest. My breath hitches, and a sting hits the back of my eyes.

His face goes serious, eyes washing over me. "I didn't reach out because I didn't want to be another voice deciding things for you."

Instead of words, I step forward and take his hand. Our fingers tangle. A low chuckle rumbles from his chest as we walk toward the same horizon.

EPILOGUE

MAVERICK

Twilight whispers across the land like a breath. Crickets soft and insistent.

The last rays of the sun glow like burnished gold against distant silhouettes, mountains cut from the same black cloth as impending night.

The land's quiet, the way only owned land can be. It isn't conquered or possessed. Nope, this land's chosen. The way it *should* be.

My muscles ache, hip joint an angry memory. A full day's work done. Steadying posts, testing line. Straightening, mending, building.

Behind me, the screen door creaks. I don't turn because I don't need to. I always feel her before I see her.

She comes up behind me, barefoot and careful, slipping her arms around my waist, cheek resting between my shoulder blades like fate carved that spot for her.

"I'm sweaty, Princess," I scold, trying to pull away. But she won't let me.

"You're sexy, Cowboy," she murmurs.

"Could say the same."

"You haven't even looked at me."

"Want to know a secret?" I drawl.

"What's that?"

"I never stop looking at you, Mia. Even when I'm halfway across the ranch. Never stop feeling you, either."

She smiles against my back.

We stand like this for a while. The hop lines darken from deep emerald to ebony as the thin, white-light of the moon scatters, stars twinkling overhead.

"Remember the first time we stargazed together?" I ask.

"I do," she answers, sliding around to face me.

My head dips, and I take her mouth. Not frantic or rushed. But slow, steady, the way I work the ranch.

Learning every line of the sinewy land. The dips where shadow shelters seedlings from the day's heat. The hidden creeks and quiet springs where green grass tufts, and pronghorns drink.

Slow work. Patient work. The kind that pays off if you don't rush it.

"My legal team called earlier…"

"And?" I ask, tensing slightly.

"Between negligence, financial mishandling, and insurance issues, Crowe is done."

"And your parents, Mia?"

She sighs, mint eyes large and fringed with thick black lashes. Moonlight kissing her face, threading white gold in her tresses.

"I saw they called, too."

She nods, frowning. "They want to help fund the audit. No strings." Her eyes cast to the side. "They apologized."

My hand comes up, brushing her cheek. I move slowly, measuring the moment.

"That what you want?"

She considers it. Then nods. "Yes. On my terms."

Pride settles deep in my chest. "But?" I ask, noticing sadness flicker behind her eyes.

She shrugs, biting her bottom lip. "Maybe part of me wants to see Crowe punished for what he did. Maybe part of me doesn't want to accept my parents' apology. Doesn't think it's enough."

I nod, pulling her close. "You want justice."

"Yes. Justice." Her voice softens. "Does that make me wrong? Or vindictive?"

I pause, letting her words settle. "I used to think justice came clean. Straight lines. Clear endings." I brush my thumb along her cheek. "Life doesn't work that way. It circles. Returns. Lets go when it's ready. Some things don't get resolved. They just stop owning you. And that's enough."

She steps closer, fingers sliding into the belt loops of my jeans, thumbs brushing skin like she's reminding herself I'm real. "Glad life circled me back to you."

"Knew it would," I confess, dipping my head to taste her.

The breeze lifts her hair, loose now, no braids today. Just sun and freedom and the faint scent of plum and roses.

"Do you ever miss it?" I ask, surveying the distant fence.

"What?"

"The roar of the crowds. The lights. The adoration."

"Not for one moment." No hesitation. "And you?"

"Thought I did ... till I met you," I confess.

"Because you need fame?" she asks.

"No, because I need to be needed. Not by everyone. Just by who matters."

"That will never change."

Our lips brush again—soft, heated. Then, our gazes stretch up to the stars, silence sealing an unspoken oath.

"You know," she says, glancing toward the barn frame we staked out, "Mrs. Everley asked what I plan to do when all this is finally over."

"And?" I ask.

Her smile is slow, knowing. "I told her I was thinking about learning how to shear alpacas."

I laugh, low and surprised. "You serious?"

"Deadly." She lifts a brow. "Think I'd be good at it."

I catch her chin, thumb brushing the curve of her jaw. "Think you'd be good at anything you choose."

My lips feather over the spot, then, down her neck. When I reach the sensitive skin where her collarbone and shoulder meet, she arches back, moaning.

"Should shower first," I murmur against her hot flesh.

"Can't wait that long, Cowboy."

Heat and pressure build at the base of my spine, breath coming faster as I continue my incremental descent toward her gorgeous breasts.

"What *can* you wait for?" I ask, dark and dangerous.

"I can make it to the couch ... *maybe*."

I chuckle, liking this game. My hands fumble with the flowing, draping folds of her sundress, bunching the fabric until I slide a hand beneath.

"No underwear?" I growl.

Mischief glints in her eyes. "Told you I can't wait."

I walk her backward toward the house, the porch boards warm beneath our feet, the door closing behind us with a soft click that feels like punctuation instead of an ending.

Inside, the light spills across the floor, dust motes floating like they've got nowhere better to be.

I take my time with her. Because now, I can.

Clothes fall where they may. Her laughter is quiet, breathless. My hands learn her again, slower this time. No edge. No cliff.

When I ease her down onto the couch, she pulls me with her, fingers tracing the circle on my chest like it's a map she's memorized. "This still us?" she whispers, warm and lazy.

"Always was."

Her legs wrap around me, strong and sure, guiding me home. Lost in her, I nearly come undone. I turn my head to the side. Squeeze my eyes shut.

Then, I move sensually, savoring everything. The hitch of her breath. The beat of her heart. The tiny tremors that tell me she's close.

"Yes," she whimpers, gripping my back.

I gasp, sinking into her again. Happily drowning.

Time dissolves. Meaning. The world. Nothing matters but her and me and this moment—warm breaths, hot kisses. Possessive fingers that go both ways.

When she shatters around me, I give her everything. Every piece of me there is to give.

Later, she rests her head on my chest, palm splayed over my heart, listening like she's counting something that finally adds up.

Outside, the wind moves through the hop lines. The fence holds. The land waits. And for the first time in my life, so do I.

When her yawns still, her body melts into mine, I rouse her.

"You'll sleep better in our bed, Princess."

"Mm hmm," she agrees drowsily, eyes heavy-lidded as I carry her down the hallway, laying her down gently.

"Where are you going?" she murmurs as I shrug into my robe, padding toward the door.

"Be back in a minute."

Outside, I search the rust-colored earth, still warm from the day, until I find the perfect pebble. River-washed smooth and thin.

I place it on the windowsill...

THE FIRST TIME I see her, she's standing in the Nevada dust with blood on her sleeve and murder in her eyes. The second time, she points a shotgun at my chest.

Fair enough.

Continue reading with Boone and Delaney's story in *Off-Limits Cowboy Bodyguard*.

NOT READY TO SAY GOODBYE to Mia and Maverick? Unlock an **exclusive bonus scene** where shared ground, open skies, and a slow ride remind them that love doesn't need an audience to be real.

JOIN THE ENGRID EAVES COMMUNITY!

ALPHA-EMOTIONAL HEROES.
HEADSTRONG, CURVY GIRLS.
SAVAGE ROMANCE.

GIVEAWAYS. FREEBIES.
NEW RELEASES. LATEST NEWS.

Subscribe to my newsletter today to never miss out on a
new steamy, small-town read.
SIGN UP FOR MY NEWSLETTER

Also by Engrid Eaves

Welcome to Rough & Ready Country

A rugged frontier of loyal cowboys, protective mountain men, dangerous firefighters, and emotionally safe alpha heroes who fall hard and forever.

If you love:

- grumpy/sunshine chemistry
- curvy heroines
- protective heroes
- forced proximity
- cowboys obsessed with their women

...then welcome home.

Rough & Ready Country

Rugged cowboys, protective mountain men, and curvy heroines who change everything.

Start with: Love at First Stranger

Read the series in Kindle Unlimited.

Rough & Ready Firefighters

Protective firefighter heroes, forced proximity, Vegas chaos, and happily-ever-afters forged in fire.

Start with: Bidding on the Cowboy Fireman

Read the series in Kindle Unlimited.

ROUGH & READY PROTECTORS

Dangerous cowboys. Protective bodyguards. Men who were never supposed to fall in love.

Start with: First-Time Cowboy Bodyguard

Shop the series in Kindle Unlimited.

DEADFALL RIDGE

Broody mountain men, forced proximity, possessive protectors, and rugged heroes willing to risk everything for love.

Start with: Rescue for the Mountain Man

Read the series in Kindle Unlimited.

BLACK COVENANT MC

Outlaw protectors. Dangerous devotion. A motorcycle club bound by loyalty, violence, and the women who bring hardened men to their knees.

Start with: Claimed by the Covenant

Read the series in Kindle Unlimited.

ALIENS OF THE STARBORN RANGE

Protective alien cowboys, Nevada Gothic mystery, ancient secrets, and fated love beneath the desert stars.

Start with: The Cowboy Alien's Fated Mate

Read the series in Kindle Unlimited.

Thank you for visiting Rough & Ready Country.

More rugged protectors, small-town heat, and happily-ever-afters are waiting just over the next mountain pass.

ABOUT THE AUTHOR

ALPHA-EMOTIONAL HEROES.
HEADSTRONG, CURVY GIRLS.
SAVAGE ROMANCE.

Bestselling author Engrid Eaves writes steamy, fast-paced romances featuring gruff alpha male protectors and the headstrong, curvy girls they fall head over heels for.

Her heroes may have painful pasts, but they always find forever with their soulmates. Sexy, satisfying, heartfelt happily ever afters guaranteed!

If you'd like to stay in touch or get your next delicious cowboy mountain man, curvy girl romance fix (and who doesn't?), sign up for her newsletter: www.engrideaves.com.

amazon.com/author/engrideaves

goodreads.com/engrideaves

bookbub.com/profile/engrid-eaves

instagram.com/engrid_eaves

tiktok.com/@authorengrideaves

facebook.com/EngridEavesAuthor